A Prodigal Return

(Book 5: An Irish Family Saga)

By

Jean Reinhardt

Historical Fiction

'We had to celebrate and rejoice, for your brother was dead but has come to life; he was lost and has been found.'
Luke 15:32

<u>Dedication</u>

To Deb, a good friend can be hard to find.
Thanks for being there.

CHAPTER ONE

Tom Gallagher had never seen his mother, Catherine, walk so fast and in spite of his long legs he was finding it difficult to keep up with her. Lily, his uncle's wife, linked his arm and did her best to match his step but she was shorter than the sixteen-year-old and ended up half walking, half running, to keep pace with him.

"Eyes ahead, Tom. Never mind what's been said on either side of the street," Lily was panting as she spoke.

She needn't have worried. The basket hanging from his mother's arm had Tom's full attention. He tried to focus on how the rhythm of her step controlled the movement of its swing but it was impossible to block out the laughter of the women behind them. The young teenager knew full well what sort of business they were in, which was why the three of them were hurrying through the street as if a pack of wolves snapped at their heels.

"Not too far now, Tom. Don't you be listening to what those hussies are shouting at you. And not a word of this to your da or your uncle, hear?"

"Yes, Ma. I hear you, but what are we doing in this part of the city?" his question went unanswered.

They rounded a corner into an alley so narrow, had they stretched out their arms, their knuckles would have scraped off the grime covered walls on either side. Catherine stopped at the first house in a terraced row and stepped through its entrance, the door long since gone to fuel someone's fire. Lily pushed Thomas ahead of her and took a quick look up and down the alley before following him into the grubby, dark hallway.

Knocking on the first door she saw, Catherine hoped they would not have to venture up the littered stairway. A young ragged child, his mouth crusted in sores, opened the door and Catherine inquired about a Mrs. Bridie McGrane. Eyeing the basket on her arm, the boy offered to show them the way.

"Well, thank you kindly, son. Lead on," Catherine stood aside to let him pass.

Tom felt bile rise in his throat at the stench of the place and swallowed hard, determined not to retch in front of anyone. He marvelled at the way his mother and Lily could just as easily have been walking through a park, by the way they carried themselves. Not once did he see them raise a hand to their nose, as he himself was eventually forced to do.

"Is your ma at home, love?" Catherine asked the young boy as he led them to the end of the hallway, towards the back of the house.

"She's dead, missus."

"Where's your father?" asked Tom.

"And who wants to know?" came a defensive reply.

"It's all right, son. We're only here to see an old friend fallen on hard times. Nobody's looking for your da," Catherine assured the boy, who had stopped in his tracks.

"That door down yonder is Mrs. McGrane's. The last one, with the wailing of a baby coming out of it," he pointed to an even narrower, darker corridor than the one they had just walked through.

Catherine dipped her hand under the blue checked cover in her basket to pull out a loaf of bread. "Good lad. Here's a little something for your trouble."

"Thanks missus," the boy's eyes lit up as he snatched the food before running back up the hallway.

Tom noticed the difference in the level of the floor and worried the house might be sloping to one side.

"I fear this building is about to fall in on top of us," he whispered to Lily from behind.

"We'll be grand, Tom. This part of the house was probably added on to the back, to fit more people in. Be thankful she's not in the basement with the pigs. In the cold weather, there's nothing like sleeping next to a nice fat sow to keep a body warm."

Tom could not see Lily's face to discern whether or not she was being serious but the tone of her voice was enough to tell him so. He had a feeling she may have been speaking from experience.

A very weak beam of daylight filtered into the narrow corridor behind them but it was enough to show up the filth and grime, the source of a very rancid odour. When they reached the last door Catherine knocked and stood back. The door creaked open to reveal a young girl, not more than eight years old, rocking a crying baby in her arms. Catherine looked over a head of matted brown hair to where three younger children huddled together on an old, badly stained mattress.

"Is Mrs. McGrane here with ye, love?" she asked softly.

The girl nodded her head and pointed to her left. Catherine gave a quick glance at Lily and Tom, before stepping into a room as grim and depressing as the rest of the building. In a dark corner lay a heap of rags, partly covered by an old torn blanket. As she bent low over the figure, it was hard to tell if the woman was breathing or not.

"Bridie. Bridie, love, do you remember me? You would have known me as Catherine McGrother."

The woman's eyelids flickered at the sound of a familiar name from her past.

"You remember me from our school days in Ireland, don't you? I used to sit behind you, Bridie. You were a mighty singer back then," Catherine knelt down on the dusty, earthen floor by the sick woman's side, "I can see you've fallen on hard times, Bridie. My parents were very sorry to hear about your mother not surviving the crossing on the boat. It must have been a terrible blow to you, arriving in a strange land at such a tender age and no family to look out for you."

"I was a bit of a wild wee thing, Catherine, and spent most of my time hiding from women who wanted to put me in a foundling home or, God forbid, send me out west on a train, with other unfortunate orphans."

"They meant well, Bridie," said Catherine. "You might have lived on a farm with decent food and fresh air. Surely that's better than sleeping in sewer pipes?"

The response was so low, Catherine had to lean close to hear what was said. Lily put a hand on her sister-in-law's shoulder to draw her back, with a warning to be careful of catching 'the fever'.

"Here, Bridie, let me help you sit up, so you can have a wee sup of this water," Catherine ignored Lily's advice. "It's grand and clean, I brought it with me – and a basket of food. I'll leave that here with your children."

"Them's not mine," came a weak reply. "The baby is. He's all I've got left. I lost my man and our two boys when our building caught fire last year, God have mercy on their poor souls," a rasping cough shook the ragged bundle and it was a couple of minutes before the woman could go on, "I didn't know I was carrying Jeremiah at the time, but it lifted my spirit when I found out. He's a good baby and I managed to earn enough money to keep us – up until a month ago."

They were interrupted by the sound of a man's voice shouting in the corridor. The speed at which the door burst open caused a cloud of fine dust to fill the room and Tom stepped in front of his mother and Lily.

A tall, broad-shouldered man with a furious scowl on his face grabbed hold of the boy's lapels and pushed him aside, "Get out, ya bunch of no-good do-gooders. Leave us alone, we're not causing any harm to anyone," he roared.

As Catherine stood to speak, her son put a hand on the man's chest and was struck squarely on the chin by a fist as hard as a rock. Staggering backwards, Tom was about to land on top of Bridie when Lily caught him by the arm. Catherine was by his side in a second and placed herself in front of her son.

"No, Francis, it's alright. I know this woman, we went to school together in Ireland," Bridie's effort in shouting out caused another bout of harsh coughing.

9

Examining the mark from the blow on Tom's face, Catherine explained that she had come to see Bridie, having heard that she was ill. Pointing to the basket of food being held by one of the children, she told him they were welcome to share it.

"We don't need no charity, ma'am. Bridie could do with the nourishment, though," the man handed the baby to Lily and gathered his children together. "I'll take them out for some fresh air and leave you to your visit. I'd prefer it if you were not here on my return, if you don't mind."

As he brushed past Tom he muttered a quick apology and when the last child had shut the door behind her, the basket could be seen standing in the middle of the floor, still full of food.

The baby had begun to whimper and Lily rocked him gently. As Bridie held out her arms to take him, Tom walked away to steal a glance through the slits in the rough wooden planks that had been nailed across the unglazed window. He knew the baby was about to be suckled and had turned away, more to save his own embarrassment than give the mother privacy.

"How did you find me, Bridie, to send that message?" asked Catherine.

"I was begging in the street and saw you pass by with your daughter. It was she that caught my eye, there was something very familiar about her. Sure, isn't she the spit of you?" Bridie never took her eyes from her baby as he suckled. "But it was when you spoke to her and I heard your accent that I knew who you were. I followed you home, did you not see me behind you?"

"No, I can't say as I did. I was most likely hurrying back for something or other. That would have been our Ellen you saw with me. She's the image of me, alright – even I can see it," Catherine smiled and offered some more water. "Who's the man with those children, Bridie, are you his woman now?"

"Not at all. Molly, his eldest girl minds the younger ones while we go out to look for work. There's three families living in this room. Francis lost his wife while she was carrying her last child, both of them died, rest their poor souls. He's afraid his children will be taken away if they're found on their own. I think he's been secretly pleased about me ailing, so that I have to stay here with them."

"Is there no one in the third family sharing with ye that can mind the children?" asked Lily.

Bridie shook her head, "They're a young couple, not long over from Belfast. I doubt they'll be here for too long, seeing as they both have regular work now. Sure I can't blame them for leaving, best they get out before any babies come along."

"Can I do anything for you, Bridie? I have a little money saved."

"That's mighty kind of you Catherine, but I fear I've not long left. There's only one thing I ask and I'll die happy if you can find it in your heart to do it."

"What is it, Bridie, do you want us to take you to a doctor?"

"No, I saw one a while back. He wasn't very hopeful either." Bridie looked straight into Catherine's eyes, "Will you take my son and raise

11

him as your own? Today, if you can, before I change my mind."

There was an awkward silence until Lily stepped forward.

"I will, if you'll let me, Bridie. I'm wed to Catherine's brother, Thomas. I can't have any children of my own, but I would dearly love to care for your son," it was blurted out impulsively but Lily meant every word.

"Wee Thomas McGrother? The teacher's pet, with all his fancy poems. Ahh, I remember him well. If you promise to do right by my child, I'll be happy to hand him over to your care," Bridie wheezed.

"We'll have none of that talk, do you hear me?" Catherine took her son by the arm, "Myself and Tom are going out to find a barrow and we'll bring you to the infirmary right this minute."

Before anyone had a chance to protest, Catherine grabbed Tom by the wrist and pulled him into the corridor. Both mother and son were silent as they made their way outside and further down the alleyway until they came to a couple of men sitting on a doorstep.

"Would you know of a barrow we could use for a few hours?" asked Catherine.

She explained why it was needed and offered to pay for its use.

"I have one, missus, but I'll push it myself, if you don't mind. That way I'll be sure of getting it back."

Tom, taking offense at what was being implied, protested that they were not thieves but his mother silenced him with a look. She thanked the man and turned to walk back to Bridie, linking her son's arm as they went.

"Come along, Tom. He knows where to find us. Let's get this poor woman and her baby away from that filthy hovel she's been living in."

CHAPTER TWO

"It kills me to see you hand over another sixpence, James," Mary smacked her husband lightly on the back of the head. "Stop leaving that donkey at the side of the road, while you're in Paddy Mac's. Do you hear me?"

Their son, Jamie, gulped down the rest of his tea and took his good jacket from a hook by the door. He looked very neat, with a freshly trimmed beard.

"You're in a mighty rush to get to Mass, aren't you? Are you sure that's where you're headed now, Jamie?" teased his father.

Mary shot her son a scornful look and received a peck on the cheek in reply.

"I'm not staying here to listen to the pair of ye squabbling over the latest fines at Petty Sessions. If you and the rest of your cronies would stay with your animals while they grazed along the ditches, ye wouldn't be handing over so many sixpences now, would ye?"

The couple smiled at one another as they listened to their son good-naturedly reprimand his father, on his way out of the house.

"He's right, though James. You could at least stay with the ass while he's grazing, couldn't you?" chided Mary, as soon as they were alone.

"What, and sit looking at him? I suppose I could always bring a bit of mending with me to keep me busy. Sure, wouldn't the hotel love to see me on the side of the road with its fine linen draped across the ditch while I stitch it," James laughed at the thought of it.

At every Petty Sessions hearing, a handful of men and women from the parish would be summoned to pay fines, for allowing their donkeys to graze unattended on the grassy verges of the public highway. This was known as grazing *'the long acre'* and cows and goats could be found doing likewise.

"I suppose it's cheaper than renting a field for the poor old donkey. Go on now, James and get ready for Mass. I think we should leave a bit earlier than usual this morning and catch our Jamie with that girl he's sweet on. Maggie has her informers keeping an eye on him," said Mary.

"Maggie is late rising this morning. Is she having another day in bed then? I hope she's not ailing. It's not like her to stay away from Mass, you know how much she looks forward to the bit of gossip."

"I did call her, but she gave out to me for waking her and pulled the quilt up over her head," said Mary.

"Speaking of gossip, did I tell you that Petey Halpin's cousin, over in Liverpool, is wed to one of our grandnieces?" said James.

"Well now, your sister was told about that on Friday, but we didn't mention it to you. It's best not to talk about such behaviour," replied Mary in a smug tone.

"I should have known Maggie would have the news got already. I suppose the girl is with child and that's what all the hurry was about," said James.

He was thinking about his own daughter, Catherine, who married her unsuspecting husband, Patrick, never telling him she was carrying another man's child – a man who had forced himself upon her. James was glad that his wife and sister had never been told that secret.

15

"Poor Owen and Rose would turn in their graves if they knew that one of their grandchildren was such a hussy. That girl was always overly friendly with men. If you ask me, she may not even know who the father of the unfortunate child is," said Mary.

"Have a bit of charity, woman, you're about to kneel in prayer up in the church. At least she's wed now. That'll put a halt to her gallop. And that young man is to be commended for doing the decent thing."

"More fool is he. But at least the innocent wee mite will have a father to put a roof over their heads and food on the table." A wistful look came over Mary's face, "James, I have a sudden longing to write a letter to our Mary-Anne. Can we do it this afternoon? We haven't heard a word from her this long time."

CHAPTER THREE

"How do I stop it crying? The neighbours will be knocking on the door any minute now. Have you prepared that bottle, yet?"

Lily turned and smiled at the sight of her husband pacing across the room, rocking a very hungry baby in his arms.

"Here you are, and he's a boy, not an 'it' and a very loud one, at that."

Thomas sat on a chair by the window, allowing the early morning sun wash over them. He was amazed at how quickly the milk was disappearing into the tiny, gulping mouth. As she folded some bedlinen, Lily smiled at the grunts and gasps of satisfaction coming from the little bundle in her husband's arms.

"I've never seen a baby put weight on so quickly. It's thanks to the good milk we've been giving him. His poor mother had barely anything in her breast but I daresay what she had was better than the filthy, watery liquid he would have received otherwise," said Lily.

"How can such a tiny infant swallow at this speed? I hope that's not a sign he'll be fond of the drink when older," laughed Thomas.

"Don't even think such a thing. You will have to set a good example for him, he's your son now. Are you not happy to have a child of your own to rear, Thomas?"

The anxious look on his wife's face told him Lily was just as nervous about the prospect of raising a child as he was.

"You of all people have no need to ask such a question of me, with my own daughter still in Ireland, refusing to leave her grandparents,"

Thomas looked down at the sleeping baby in his arms. "It will take me a bit of time to feel like a father to this wee mite, but I'll admit he has already found a place in my heart."

Thomas had tried on numerous occasions over the years to bring Eliza to America, having left her as a young baby in his parent's care, after the death of her mother. Losing his wife at such a young age had been unbearable for Thomas, so when the offer of work on a newspaper in New York came up he saw it as a fresh start. At first, Eliza was to remain in Ireland until Thomas had settled into his new life, but as the years went by he could see on each of his visits that it would be wrong to separate his daughter from her grandparents.

"Eliza is a young woman now, my love. I could see in her eyes how much she enjoyed her last trip over. Do you recall how she spoke of her childhood friends who have come to live here? I daresay it won't be too long before we have her join us, Thomas. But in the meantime, this young fella will keep us from idleness. Is that not so, Jeremiah?" Lily kissed the sleeping baby's head and carefully took him from her husband's arms.

Thomas looked at the expression of maternal love on his wife's face and knew that she had done the right thing in bringing into their home a young baby sorely in need of caring guardians. He could see that Lily was already a mother to her newly adopted son and was sure that he, himself, would soon begin to think of the young child as his own flesh and blood.

The apartment they had recently moved to was in a good area and had two large bedrooms, plenty of space to accommodate an extra family member. Thomas knew that as long as his mother was alive, his daughter would remain in Ireland, she had more or less told him so on her last visit to New York. In spite of that, Thomas wished his mother a long and healthy life, he had plenty to fill his time while he waited, especially with a baby to take care of and provide for.

"Lily, I've been meaning to discuss something with you, and I think now might be as good a time as any," Thomas whispered.

"There's no need to speak so softly, my love, Jeremiah will remain asleep once his belly is full. What is it? You have such a frown upon your face, I'm not sure I want to hear what you have to say."

"There was more in that letter from home than I shared with you at the time, Lily. I cannot divulge the content just yet, but Mr. McIntyre feels it worth investigating," Thomas was speaking of his employer, "He feels that an Irishman will have a much better chance of becoming privy to information not easily acquired. I would receive a fine commission to add to our savings, Lily, and with our new addition to the family the money would be very welcome. Do you not agree?"

"Oh Thomas, the last time you accepted an assignment like that you were away for such a long time – and you put your life in danger. Must you do the same again?"

"Don't fret so, Lily. There will be some element of risk but you know how careful I am," Thomas turned his back to his wife and looked down two floors onto the street below. "And yes, I will have to travel quite a distance for this particular assignment. I really cannot say too much about it for now, but a young man I know from the past may have gotten himself into a bit of trouble."

As Lily kept her eyes on the broad back of the man who meant everything to her, mixed emotions prevented her from speaking. She knew that if she begged him not to go, Thomas would abide by her wishes but it would hang between them and there would come a day when he would resent the restrictions put upon him. Lily had made a vow to herself never to hold her husband back from the work he loved most – fighting injustice and exposing corruption.

"How long might you be gone, Thomas?"

"I cannot say for sure, love, but I promise I shall not stay away a minute longer than is necessary."

Thomas left his place by the window and pulled a chair up in front of the one his wife was now seated upon.

"You must promise that you will not be overly anxious about me whilst I am away." He took both her hands in his. "Can you do that, love?"

As she looked him straight in the eye, Lily smiled warmly and nodded, "Of course I can promise that, Thomas, sure I'll have a young baby to keep me busy. I may not even notice your absence."

Thomas laughed and wrapped his arms snugly around Lily's shoulders. He knew that she was putting on a brave face to reassure him and that she would worry every night before falling asleep until his return, and he loved her all the more for her pretence.

CHAPTER FOUR

As the eight-year-old boy scrutinized the horizon he seemed unaware of a hand lightly stroking his raven-black hair. This was something he would normally shrug off indignantly, embarrassed by the public show of affection.

"Why if it isn't Mary-Anne McGrother," a female voice called out, "What brings you back to Ireland? I hope none of the family are poorly."

The boy spun quickly around at the mention of a familiar name and moved closer to Mary-Anne, who was struggling to remember the name of the middle aged woman beaming at her.

"Oh it's yourself, Mrs. Murphy. I'm sorry it took me so long to recognize you but it's been a long time since I was last home. Nobody is sick, thank goodness." Mary-Anne shot a glance at the boy but he had turned once more to watch out for the first sign of land.

The woman chuckled. "I haven't been back myself for almost three years. My youngest girl still lives in Blackrock, she got wed to one of the Breens. He's a fisherman of course, as are most of the men in the village. Do you remember how your brother-in-law fished our boat for us after I lost my two boys, rest their poor souls? A good hearted man, is Patrick Gallagher, no doubt about it," a wistful look came over the woman's face, "Well, I gave that boat to my daughter as a wedding present and they moved into my old wreck of a house. I was happy to leave Blackrock, too many sad memories there for me."

"So you live in England now, Mrs. Murphy?"

"In Manchester, love. It's a grand place, my eldest daughter wed an Englishman, a grocer with his own shop, no less." Mrs. Murphy leaned in close to whisper. "A Protestant, mind you, but he's not very pious and the children are all Catholic, thanks be to God."

"How many grandchildren do you have altogether?" Mary-Anne tried to keep the conversation away from her own circumstances.

"Three in Manchester that I live with, above the grocers. I look after them while their mother helps her husband with the shop. My fifth grandchild is expected any day now, that's why I'm on my way over – to be with my youngest when the time comes for her second baby to arrive. I was with her when she had the first one. A girl wants her mother by her side at a time like that. Does this fine young man belong to yourself, Mary-Anne? What a grand head of hair, as black as coal it is."

"I'm his guardian, I cared for his poor mother until she died, rest her soul. He was such a tiny baby and sickly at that."

"Did you marry over in England? Only, I don't recall hearing about it myself. You know how quickly news travels back and forth across the water."

Mary-Anne shook her head. "I had no time for that sort of thing, Mrs. Murphy. My mistress was never blessed with children of her own and was happy to have one to play with when she felt up to it – she wasn't in the best of health, herself. So, when his mother passed, I was allowed to have the poor wee mite with me. I tell you, I was kept going from morn till night. But I'm sure you would know all about that yourself, with a house full of wee ones to take care off."

"Nan," a child's excited voice broke into their conversation. "I can see land, are we almost there?"

As she peered into the distance, Mary-Anne's heart began to beat a little faster. She could see small boats just ahead and knew it wouldn't be too long before the steam packet docked. The excitement and anticipation beginning to rise inside her surprised the normally calm and controlled young woman.

"How much longer, Nan?" Mary-Anne felt a tug on her sleeve.

"Not too long now, young man," Mrs. Murphy said.

The years rolled back for Mary-Anne as the ship entered Dundalk Bay and the realization of what lay ahead hit home. The one trip her parents had made over to see her, a year after she had left home, had not resulted in a happy reunion. Her father had accused her of putting on 'airs and graces' and her mother cried for most of the afternoon they had spent together. It had been a relief for Mary-Anne to wave them off as they boarded the train to Manchester. Any letters she subsequently received from her parents or siblings, with even a hint of another visit, all received the same answer – she had too many commitments and responsibilities to spare the time, either to receive visitors or make the trip home.

Mary-Anne was becoming anxious about the kind of welcome she might receive, arriving unannounced on her parents' doorstep with a child in tow. She would soon find out that her father and mother were the least of her worries.

CHAPTER FIVE

Nobody had heard a word from Thomas McGrother since his departure to an undisclosed place. Lily was beginning to worry, in spite of his reassurances that there would be very little danger involved in his latest assignment. Having promised to send a message home once a week, Thomas had failed to do so.

"Not once, Catherine," Lily blew into her handkerchief. "Not even one telegram and there should have been at least four by now."

"Sit down, love. You're wearing a hole in my best rug with your pacing up and down. Here, take the baby and let me get us a cup of tea," said Catherine.

As the table was being laid Patrick came through the door, a worried look on his face. The two women watched as he removed his cap and jacket.

"Well? What did Mr. McIntyre have to say for himself?" asked Lily.

Patrick sat at the table across from her, his broad calloused hands encircling an empty cup. Knowing that she would see through any attempt to hide his concern made it difficult for him to look his sister-in-law in the eye.

"Nobody at the paper has heard a word from Thomas since he left. He was supposed to keep in touch with Mr. McIntyre," Patrick stared at the ribbon of amber liquid being poured into his cup.

"I'm sorry the tea's a bit weak, yet. I'll leave it stew a while," Catherine apologised.

"I knew there was something wrong, I could feel it in my bones," cried Lily jumping up from her seat. "Did he tell you where he sent Thomas? We shall have to go to the police about this."

The look Patrick shot her before replying to Lily's question gave Catherine a knot in her stomach. She was hoping Mr. McIntyre could tell them where her brother had been sent but in her heart she knew what the answer would be.

"I'm sorry, Lily, but nobody has any clue as to Thomas's whereabouts. It wasn't his boss that sent him on that assignment – it was him that informed Mr. McIntyre about it and said he would like to take it on."

"Then we must go to the police, Patrick. Right away, this minute," Lily was putting on her coat, her hat already perched on the side of her head.

"No, Lily, we can't do that. Not yet anyway. Mr. McIntyre is afraid that it might make things worse for Thomas if the police are involved. He feels sure the reason we've not heard anything is because it's not safe for him to send a telegram or mail a letter."

Catherine had joined her sister-in-law in pacing the floor, rocking the sleeping baby as she did so. The noise of the street below filled a terrible silence that had fallen upon the room. A door banging somewhere in the building brought the three of them out of their anxious thoughts.

"We can't just sit around and do nothing, Patrick."

"I know, Catherine. I know," Patrick stood in front of Lily, putting a halt to her frantic pacing, and looked her straight in the eye. "You should stay here with us for a while, Thomas would want you to do that, Lily. I have someone in mind that might shed a bit of light on this 'secret' assignment."

25

Tears streamed down her face as Lily looked with a small measure of hope into his eyes and all she could manage was a nod. As the door closed behind him, Patrick felt bad for lying to the two women but it was the only bit of consolation he could give them. Not one name came to mind of anyone who might know the whereabouts of his brother-in-law but there was a place where he could begin his search. It was not somewhere he would normally frequent and he wasn't even sure of the welcome he would receive when he got there.

By the time Patrick arrived at his destination he was soaked to the skin. There had been no work for him nor any of the other quarry workers that day, on account of the heavy rain, so Tom had worn his father's oilskin coat to his work as an apprentice typesetter – a position his uncle Thomas had recently secured for him at Mr. McIntyre's newspaper.

A hot stove was positioned in the centre of MacNeill's bar and Patrick nodded at one or two familiar faces as he worked his way toward the source of heat. The smell of damp work clothes, cigarette smoke and alcohol brought back memories of days in Blackrock, when the weather prevented men from fishing or labouring in the fields. Patrick closed his eyes briefly, standing as close to the heat as possible, and let his thoughts go back to Ireland.

"The heat's not free, it'll cost you the price of a drink," the barman shouted over the hum of male voices.

Patrick ordered a beer and pushed through the steaming mass until he reached the bar. He recognized the man serving him from the odd occasion he had accompanied Thomas to the premises. It was a place where his brother-in-law gathered information not easily available to journalists or the law. The barman was a good source and if anyone knew the whereabouts of Thomas, it would be him.

"Do I know you?" asked the barman as he served him.

Patrick thanked him and drank half the contents of the tankard in one go before giving him his name.

"Thomas not with you today? Off investigating something or other, is he?" the look of surprise on Patrick's face made the barman laugh. "Before you even said who you were it came to me. Don't have the pleasure of your company too much in here, do we?"

Deciding to be honest in the hope of gaining the man's confidence Patrick explained why he was not a regular visitor.

"I made a promise to my wife that if we came to America I would not get overly involved with politics – or drink. Difficult as it is, I've been keeping my word, most of the time."

"Well, it's the first time I've seen you in here without Thomas. I must get another barrel from the cellar, it has been mighty busy in here today, what with the bad weather and all. Could I trouble you to help me bring it up?"

"Off course I will, sure I'm well used to lifting heavy weights. I'm a quarryman. It's why I have no work on such a wet day as this."

"I know you are, Thomas introduced you as one the first time he brought you here."

Amazed at the memory of the man, Patrick followed him down into a dark cellar and shivered as the coolness hit his damp clothes. He waited while the barman rolled barrels from one side to another, eventually selecting the one he needed to bring up the rough, wide steps they had just descended.

"Has Thomas come by here at any time over the last few weeks?" Patrick inquired.

"Can you not ask him that yourself? Or have you two had a disagreement over something?"

"No. I haven't seen nor heard from him this past month and neither has his wife. I was hoping he might have told you about any trips he was planning on taking."

The barman had been leaning over a barrel, inspecting the iron band holding it together. He slowly straightened up and turned to face Patrick, placing both hands on his hips. He was a good six inches taller than him and the younger man found himself looking up at someone at least ten years his senior.

"How old do you think I am?" asked the barman.

"Forty-five?" Patrick didn't want to offend this giant of a man by adding years to him he didn't have.

"Add ten more onto that. And do you know how I came to this grand old age without any broken bones or knife wounds, in spite of running an establishment such as this one?" asked the barman.

"Because you're the size of Fionn Mac Cumhaill," Patrick replied, referring to a giant-sized Irish folk hero.

A hearty laugh burst from deep within the belly of the big man and he held out a hand broader and more calloused than Patrick's. The firm handshake was crushing but reassuring to the younger man.

"You've no need to fear me, Patrick. I would trust your brother-in-law with my life, he's done me some good favours over the years. Thomas must be in serious trouble if you haven't heard from him. I suspect the information you seek can be found at Tammany Hall, for that is where he was headed the last I saw of him – but you did not hear that from me. Understand? Now, don't go asking me any more questions."

Patrick nodded and thanked the man for his help, his hopes raised that finally he would get some answers as to the whereabouts of his brother-in-law.

******

It wasn't the snores and groans coming from the other bunks that kept Thomas awake, nor his aching back and weary limbs. He massaged his tired eyes with calloused palms, and tried to keep in check the flood of despair threatening to extinguish any flame of hope left in his heart.

Thomas sat up straight to stretch his spine and reminded himself that all was not lost. He had accomplished what he had set out to do and was ready to take the next step. Trying to see what condition his palms were in, Thomas squinted at them in the weak moonlight filtering into the cramped wooden shed, home to thirty other men of various ages.

The thought of his family seeing the rough, calloused hands that had been used for most of his life in the forming of words on paper, brought a smile to Thomas's face and that in itself served to lift his spirit. The weeks of hacking at rock with

29

a pick and pushing stone laden carts had taken more out of him than the other men, most of whom were used to a life of hard labour.

The work in itself was not completely to blame for the sorry condition Thomas and his fellow workers found themselves in. It was the lack of nourishing food that contributed to their weakened state. Thin broths and stale bread could not fuel a body for such strenuous labour and Thomas tried to remember how many times he had eaten meat since his arrival at the mine. He could count it on one hand but knew there was no use in complaining – he had seen what happens to anyone brave enough to speak up about the conditions they were being kept in.

Those willing to confide in Thomas had shared stories that not only made him fear for his own safety but confirmed rumours circulating among those drunk enough to spread them in the saloons of the nearest town. Had it not been for the sake of a young man's freedom, Thomas would have turned and headed for home. Instead, he voluntarily put himself in the clutches of a man whose evil reputation lingered on in the city of New York, many years after his departure.

CHAPTER SIX

Mary-Anne sat on the cart with Mrs. Murphy and her son-in-law and smiled as the young boy by her side asked question after question about the sights around him, on the two mile journey to Blackrock. She had forgotten how busy Dundalk port could be and the offer of a ride home had been gratefully accepted.

'I've plenty of money to keep us going,' thought Mary-Anne. *'But I will need every farthing, if I'm to carry out my plan.'*

If there was one thing she would always be grateful to her father for, it was his insistence that all of his children learn to read and write. Having such a skill meant that Mary-Anne's financial security would never be left to chance or the whims of an unreliable employer. She had prepared herself for the day when her ailing mistress would no longer have need of the young boy as a substitute child, in place of the babies she had miscarried.

Every penny earned was carefully deposited into a bank account and a solicitor had drawn up a document that would ensure a good financial reward should Mary-Anne be asked to leave the household. That day came sooner than expected with the sudden death of Doctor Gilmore's wife.

The night before the funeral, a tapping on her bedroom door broke into Mary-Anne's sleep and she woke up with a start. The shallow, even breathing of the young child lying beside her told her the noise had not disturbed him. Upon opening the door, she was surprised to find Doctor Gilmore standing in the dimly lit hallway of the servants' quarters and her stomach churned.

The fact that he might be renewing his nocturnal visits to her room was something Mary-Anne had not been prepared for, especially since he had made it quite clear a year before that one of the younger domestics was far more interesting and accommodating. *'Besides, you've become quite the boring old spinster of late,'* the doctor's words had stung Mary-Anne in spite of the relief she felt at his lack of interest in her.

It had been a long time since he had told her to *'Put that child to bed in the scullery maid's room'* – the meaning of which Mary-Anne understood very well indeed. Unwilling to put up with her employer's renewed interest in her, the next morning she quickly packed up her belongings and moved out with her young ward, leaving a note of resignation for Doctor Gilmore.

Thankful the young boy's chatter had distracted Mrs. Murphy for the entire journey, Mary-Anne was surprised to hear a familiar voice cut into her thoughts as the cart came to a halt.

"Why, if it isn't yourself, Miss McGrother. It is still Miss, I take it?"

"It is indeed, Paddy Mac. And I intend for it to stay that way. Sure men are just a pile of trouble, with the exception of this little man," Mary-Anne offered the boy to the man's outstretched arms. "This is the proprietor of a public house where my father and my brother spend far too much of their time – and money. Say good afternoon to Mr. MacMahon, George."

"Well you're a fine young fella and that's for sure. Have you travelled here all by yourself or are your parents about?" Paddy Mac glanced at a pony and trap that had pulled in behind the cart.

"George's poor mother died when he was a baby, rest her soul, and I became his legal guardian. Now, if you'll excuse us, we must be getting along, our trunks shall be arriving soon. Good day to you Paddy."

"Good bye, Mr. MacMahon. It was nice to meet you," young George held out a hand.

"You have much better manners than your guardian, son," Paddy Mac took the small hand and shook it firmly.

George felt a coin press into his palm and curled his fingers into a tight fist as his hand was released.

"Not much has changed here since my last visit," Mary-Anne muttered, steering her young ward across the street and towards the end of the village. She was eager to get to her parents cottage before word of their arrival reached her family.

Rounding a bend in the road, Mary-Anne could see the bent figure of a woman at work in her tiny front garden. The little house looked tired, its bare stone walls peeping through the aged whitewash. The peeling red half-door had also paid the price for its uninterrupted view of the sea and Mary-Anne felt a burning shame for her family's public display of hard times. *'What must the inside look like?'* she thought.

Before they even reached the equally neglected front gate, the middle-aged woman straightened her back, groaning softly. Mary-Anne hoped she would turn immediately and stood waiting, a tight grip on the young boy's wrist. She had warned him not to make a sound and put a finger to her

33

lips as a reminder. He responded with a wily smile, feeling like a fox about to pounce on its prey.

As the seconds flew by, Mary-Anne worried that she would be seen by anyone who might be inside the house, so she called out softly to the woman standing on the other side of the gate massaging her aching back.

"Ma, it's me. I've come home."

George had never heard that soft tone of voice directed at anyone but himself and he knew instantly, whoever this woman was, she must be very special to his guardian.

Mary McGrother held her breath as she slowly turned to face her second eldest daughter. An awkwardness came over Mary-Anne that took her by surprise, making her feel uncomfortable and at a disadvantage. She had hoped to surprise her mother but never expected the reunion to have such a strange effect on herself. Tears filled her normally cool and calculating eyes, as she allowed herself to be wrapped up in the familiar embrace of her mother's arms.

The older woman's cries of joy brought a young woman running from the house, her face full of worry and concern. She didn't know who the visitor was but noticed straight away the tight grip on the young boy's wrist. He seemed to be grimacing in pain as he tried to break free, twisting his arm and pulling back from the two crying women.

Placing her hands on Mary-Anne's shoulders, Mary stretched out her arms and held her daughter's watery gaze.

"You did mean that you're home for good, my darlin'? I heard it in your voice. Please tell me this is not merely a visit."

'My mother is the only one who can see right into my soul.' The thought was unnerving but comforting at the same time and Mary-Anne nodded her head in reply, not trusting herself to speak in case her voice should crack with emotion.

At the same time as Mary noticed George, wriggling by her daughter's side, Mary-Anne saw the young woman standing behind her mother. Both women quickly wiped their teary cheeks and turned their attention away from each other.

"And who's this young fella, trying so desperately to escape from your grasp, Mary-Anne?"

"This is George, you're grandson," came a flat reply.

Unsettling thoughts raced through Mary's head. *'She got wed and never told us. But where's her husband? Oh, bless us and save us, my daughter had a child out of wedlock. Ah no, of course not – her husband is probably working and couldn't spare the time to come with them.'*

"Before his mother died she asked me to take him in. She was all alone in the world, poor woman. I'm his guardian, so that makes you his grandmother, of sorts, does it not?"

Relief spread through Mary, silencing her anxious thoughts and she bent down to scoop up the child in her arms.

Barely able to lift him a couple of inches from the ground, Mary winced as an old familiar pain stabbed at her spine.

"Welcome to the family, George. I'm not as spritely as I used to be, otherwise I would have you bundled up in my arms right now. So you'll have to make do with a kiss and a cuddle."

The young boy squirmed as his cheeks were covered in kisses and the breath almost squeezed from his lungs. Mary-Anne intervened and rescued him, asking to be introduced to the visitor.

"Oh, Annie isn't a visitor. She lives with us. Our Jamie got himself a wife and a fine one at that," Mary held her arms out to the young woman, who seemed very uncomfortable in Mary-Anne's presence.

"Annie, this is my daughter, Mary-Anne, and it seems she's come home."

That old feeling of jealousy stabbed at Mary-Anne but she smiled sweetly and took hold of the outstretched hand. The skin felt rough to the touch and didn't match the fresh young face of its owner. The jealousy quickly turned to smugness as Mary-Anne realised her own hands were much softer and could have belonged to a lady of means.

"Well, I cannot believe any woman would be desperate enough to wed my wee brother. I hope you've made a man of him and a good one at that, although I very much doubt it."

This was the old Mary-Anne that her family were used to but it caused her mother to protectively tighten her grip on Annie's shoulders. She loved her daughter with all her heart and bit her tongue so as not to humiliate her in front of her young ward.

"Now, now, Mary-Anne. Jamie is a fine young man and a good husband to Annie. You and your brother will have to put your differences aside, if there's to be peace between us all. I'm sorry we never told you of his marriage but he made us promise not to."

"I take it they live here with you, Ma? So there will be no room for myself – or your grandson. I had best be off to find a room in a lodging house, so."

As Mary-Anne turned her mother grabbed hold of her arm and pulled her towards the house. It was at that moment the bent figure of a woman appeared just inside the doorway and a brash voice shouted out to them.

"Aha, the Prodigal has returned. I see you haven't changed a bit, Mary-Anne," Maggie was leaning on two sticks, a scowl covering the deep lines etched into her face.

"Well, if it isn't my favourite aunt. I would run into your arms and embrace you, if I didn't fear it would knock you right off your feet. How are your poor legs these days, Aunt Maggie? Buckling under all that weight I imagine."

"Mary-Anne, mind your tongue, girl. That is no . . ."

A deep hearty laugh from the older woman stopped Mary in mid-sentence and she was relieved to hear her daughter join in with the laughter. The icy atmosphere had finally broken and everyone made their way into the house, except young George, who wasn't quite sure what to make of the situation.

"Come on inside, young man. There's no need to be afraid of me," assured Maggie, gesturing for him to join them. "You'll be hearing a lot more talk like that between your mother and myself, so you may as well get used to it."

"I'm his guardian, Aunt Maggie, not his mother."

The older woman looked at her niece with a caustic eye, "Of course you are, my dear, of course you are."

CHAPTER SEVEN

As heavy rain beat against the window pane, Patrick adjusted the position of his head, allowing the caress of Catherine's warm breath to brush across his neck. Thick drapes blocked out any light from the street and prevented the heat of their bedroom escaping. It was the time of evening he loved most and normally his thoughts would sweep him into pleasant dreams full of hope and promise. Not so on this particular night.

The years they had spent in America had mostly been good to the young Irish family. There were lots of hard times, of course, as there are in most people's lives, but there was a freedom in their new country that had never been afforded them in Ireland. The work that many of the men were employed in was demanding and at times quite dangerous. If a man was careful and kept his wits about him, he could be sure of providing enough to keep a roof over his head and put good food on the table for his family. If he had a wife who was industrious and thrifty, there might even be enough money for a half decent education for some, if not all, of their children.

Catherine's face was in darkness but Patrick could tell by the rhythm of her breathing that she was awake. He tried to keep his own breath at a slow even pace, feigning sleep, in the hope that she would not ask him another question about her brother. If she thought he was in a deep sleep, his wife would never wake him up unnecessarily, knowing he had an early start for work next morning.

"It wasn't true what you told Lily about our Thomas this evening, was it?"

Patrick ignored the question.

"Don't be pretending you're asleep, I know you're lying here as anxious as myself, Patrick Gallagher."

He turned to face his wife in the darkness and knew exactly where to find her lips. Patrick felt they needed something to distract them or they would never be able to sleep and morning was just a few hours away. Love-making was the furthest thing from Catherine's mind.

"And that won't stop me questioning you, either," the words hit him like a bucket of cold water.

Patrick rolled onto his back and groaned, there would be no sleep for either of them and he may as well accept it. He knew that Catherine would imagine all sorts of desperate scenarios about what could have happened to her brother, if she felt he was hiding something from her. His own thoughts were bad enough, with the meagre amount of information he had managed to garner.

"I had to tell her something, Catherine. Poor Lily is driven demented over Thomas's disappearance and she has that wee baby to care for," Patrick whispered.

"So you lied to her. I knew it by the look on your face, even before you opened your mouth to answer her questions. Have you no news at all, Patrick?"

A long sigh filled the air around them, "Not a whisper. It's as if he's disappeared into thin air. That barman at MacNeill's knows something I'll wager, but I have to win his confidence first. You know yourself how suspicious that crowd can be," Patrick reached out, searching for Catherine's hand and felt his own being grabbed, "Give it time, love. We must keep our hopes up, for Lily's sake," he tried to reassure.

Catherine wiped tears from her face before drawing closer to Patrick. She moulded her body to his familiar shape and felt the change take place in him.

'*At least one of us should get some sleep tonight,*' she thought.

CHAPTER EIGHT

The two men basked in the fresh rays of an early morning sun, their eyes following a steam packet ship sailing out of the bay. As their boat rocked gently in the calm sea, James savoured the quietness surrounding him.

"We'll have hell to pay when we get back," his companion groaned, straightening out his arms and cracking his elbows.

"Ach, Jamie. Why did you have to go and spoil my wee bit of peace and quiet?"

"Sorry, Da. I was thinking out loud – but it's true. There'll be a price to pay for fishing on a Sunday."

James cast an eye over the bucket of fish that sat accusingly between them. For a moment he wondered if the pleasure gained from breaking what he believed to be an insignificant rule, had been worth it. It didn't take him long to decide.

"Jamie boy, when you've been wed as long as I have you'll come to realise that life will be far easier if you let your wife think she's captain of the ship. But when it comes to fishing and taking out a boat, your ma knows better than to cross me – even if it is the *Lord's Day*. Do you get my meaning, son?"

The younger man nodded allowing a sentimental smile to escape. Growing up in the McGrother household had been a very pleasant experience for Jamie. When times were hard and food scarce, his mother's hugs, embarrassing as they were, became more frequent – as did his father's ruffling of his dark brown hair.

Looking back, Jamie found it difficult to remember the grumbling hunger pains or the cold

42

gnawing at his bones, on nights when the turf had to be spared for the next day's cooking. The childhood memories filling his head were of fishing with his father and the light hearted banter between his mother and aunt. On a stormy night, when no boat could venture out, there was nothing more entertaining than the old family stories the adults would remind each other of, crying and laughing over them as if the events had just recently taken place.

Jamie was brought back to the present by the weight of his father's hand resting on his shoulder.

"You're a good man, Jamie. I'm proud to say I've raised a good man in you. I don't tell you that often enough, son."

Clearing his throat, the young fisherman nodded. A wave of guilt came over him as he recalled the previous night's conversation with his wife. Annie had made arrangements for them to lodge with a neighbour while Mary-Anne and her young ward remained in the McGrother house.

"Our visitors appear to be settling in for a long stay, Da, so I'll be taking a room with the O'Neills for a while until we find a place of our own. Annie has already paid them for tonight's bed and board. It's about time we gave you back your house, you'll be able to sleep in your own bed again," Jamie poked around in the bucket of fish, not wanting to look his father in the eye.

The older man was silent as he processed this unexpected news. It shouldn't have surprised him, as the strained relationship between his two children had intensified to a point where Jamie now left the house whenever Mary-Anne stepped through the door. His son could barely sleep under the same roof as his older sister.

"Your ma was only saying to me the other night how cosy it is sleeping in the parlour, it's the warmest room in the house. There's no need for you and Annie to leave, son. Sure it won't be long before Mary-Anne finds somewhere for herself and the boy. I'll wager that one has enough money saved to buy a wee house of her own."

"It's Annie I'm thinking of," Jamie lied. "She needs her own home. There's far too many women in that kitchen now. Do you not agree with me, Da?"

Not waiting for a reply, the young man picked up his oars and said, "Speaking of that, my stomach is beginning to grumble, I daresay there's a meal already waiting for us."

"Not to worry, son, I left a message for your ma on the table, she'll have seen it by now I'll wager."

As his mother couldn't read, Jamie wondered how she would understand the message and it bothered him that he hadn't thought to do the same for his own wife. He feared she would think him callous to leave the house in the early hours of a Sunday morning and not tell her where he was off to.

"I didn't think to do the same for Annie. Ma will give her the note to read out and I'll have to face the wrath of two women on my return," groaned Jamie.

"I didn't leave a note, son. I spread a little flour on the table and drew the shape of a boat in it. Sure that's as good as any words on a piece of paper."

As the men's laughter rang out over the still water, James picked up his oars and nodded towards the shoreline. "I suppose you're right, we had best be getting back. Poor old Lobster Hughes will think we've sailed all the way to America in his boat."

"He won't mind, Da. Sure he's well used to me taking it out now without him. Why, he told me only the other day that I would own it outright myself by the end of the year. Is that not a grand thing altogether, Da? Our own boat."

Jamie had been making regular payments to one of their elderly neighbours who was no longer fit enough to go out in his boat.

Father and son rowed in unison, a comfortable rhythm born from years of practice.

"Yours, not ours, Jamie. I've enough work as a stone mason to keep me going but you have a young wife to provide for now and in time, please God, a house full of children. Besides, you've paid for this boat with your own money and I'm proud as punch of you for doing so," James glanced over his shoulder to look his son in the eye. "You could have drunk and gambled it away, as many of your young friends have done. And sure, who could blame you? Life is hard and I sometimes wonder if I should have encouraged you to be more frivolous. You've such an old head on your young shoulders, Jamie."

"Would you ever turn around and get on with the rowing, Da," the young man was feeling uncomfortable with the look on his father's face. "There'll be no slacking on my boat, not even for family."

"I pity your crew, Jamie McGrother. You're a hard task master."

Not another word passed between the two men until they reached the shore and pulled the boat up onto the compact sand. The sky was bright and the few clouds that hung lazily above the gently rolling waves showed no sign of spilling rain upon them. The two men greeted some children who were playing on the rocks and had stopped their game momentarily, to wave at them.

As they passed by the open doors and half-doors of the houses lining the main street, the aroma of bacon and cabbage, boiled together in the same pot, taunted the men's empty stomachs. By the time they had arrived on their own doorstep, no amount of female berating could dampen their spirits. The worst thing that could have happened, was if all that remained of their Sunday meal was its smell.

CHAPTER NINE

Tammany Hall was as imposing to Patrick on the inside as it was on the outside and he resorted to a lifelong nervous habit of twisting his cap in his hands. It made him even more self-conscious that any time a young woman bustled past him, she cast an eye over his tired suit. He could see by their walk, the confidence that city life had instilled in them and wondered if his own daughters had the same air about them.

"Mr. Gallagher, Mr. Whelan will see you now. Follow me, please."

The young man walking three steps ahead of Patrick strode through the building like a lord of the manor, his chin jutting out on a head that nodded graciously at anyone who as much as glanced in his direction. Patrick checked his own posture and found that his shoulders were rounded and his head slightly bowed. Straightening himself up to his full height, it pleased him to see he was a least two inches taller than the young man in front of him.

'I'm as good as any of them,' Patrick reminded himself as they came to a halt in front of a dark panelled door.

A muffled voice responded to the three sharp raps against the solid wood. As the door swung open, Patrick found himself in an overly warm room, facing a large, dark oak desk. The young man who had escorted him, announced his arrival to an elderly, silver-haired man, whose head was bent over some papers. He waved his hand as a signal to be left alone with Patrick and then gestured toward a low chair in front of his desk, all this without as much as an upward glance.

As Patrick stared at the crown of thinning hair facing him, he was conscious of drops of perspiration soaking into his shirt. A combination of the heat in the room and his own anxiety almost forced him to remove his jacket but just as he was about to do so, the man he had come to see finally lifted his head.

"Mr. Gallagher, I hope I haven't made you feel uncomfortable. You'll have to forgive my manners, ignoring you like that."

"I know you're a very busy man, Mr. Whelan, and I'm much obliged that you could spare the time for me – so I'll get straight to the point," Patrick cleared his throat before continuing.

"No need to explain. I have read your petition and I'm sorry to tell you that I have no news for you – at least nothing you have not found out for yourself. You're brother-in-law is quite well known to us here at Tammany. I've had a number of disagree.... ahem.... discussions.... with him over the years. We don't often see eye to eye on political matters, if you understand what I mean, Mr. Gallagher."

Patrick nodded, he knew that Thomas was not easily influenced and could imagine the conversations that would have taken place between the two men.

"I'm at a loss, sir, as to who I should turn to next. I do not wish to approach the police at this time, for fear it could.... eh.... make matters worse for Thomas. I had hoped you might be able to point me in the direction of someone who.... who could help me in.... em....," Patrick silently cursed his faltering speech.

"In a discreet way?" the older man spoke softly.

Fanning himself with his cap, Patrick nodded gratefully and looked around the room. His eyes came to rest on a jug of water and some glasses sitting on a silver tray.

Mr. Whelan stood up from his desk and walked over to the matching oak sideboard to pour out two glasses of water.

"I must apologize for the window being closed but I have only recently recovered from a bout of gripe. I fear the air outside is a little too fresh for me at the moment, or so my good wife tells me. Are you a married man?" Patrick affirmed with a nod and took the proffered glass. "Then you know how wives tend to fuss over their husbands, do you not?"

"I do, sir, and that's the reason I've come here to see you. Thomas's wife, Lily, is beside herself with worry. I promised her I would do my best to find out what's become of him."

The older man circled the desk and came to a halt in front of the sun filled window. Closing his eyes, he allowed the rays of heat to warm his back, while Patrick drained his glass dry.

"I take it you are of the same political bent as your brother-in-law?"

The question threw Patrick and he wasn't sure if he should answer truthfully or not. Glancing at the other man's face he could see that the eyes were still closed but he couldn't shake the feeling of being scrutinized.

"For the most part, I am, sir. But my work keeps me far too busy to get involved in anything political these days. And my wife doesn't always approve of Thomas's way of looking at things – if you know what I mean – sir," it was an almost honest answer.

A long, tired sigh escaped from the older man as he returned to his seat opposite Patrick.

"I'm going to be completely honest with you, Mr. Gallagher, and you may take or leave what I have to say. Your brother-in-law is very good at covering his tracks when the need arises. I know this from past experience with.... let us say, negative reactions, to some of his very public opinions. If I were you, I would be sitting in front of his editor's desk at this moment asking the same questions of *him*. Do you understand what I'm trying to tell you, Mr. Gallagher?"

Patrick nodded and the feeling of running around in circles became even stronger but he was at a loss as to who might be hiding what.

"Pardon me if this seems ill-mannered on my part, sir, but you seem to be speaking in riddles. Are you telling me that Thomas is in hiding because of some form of danger? Are you implying that his editor might be involved?"

Mr. Whelan placed both hands on top of the papers on his desk and leaned forward, elbows bent. A slight flush of pink coloured his cheeks and Patrick knew immediately he had spoken out of turn.

"I never *imply* anything, young man, and you keep that in mind when you leave this building. Are we clear?" It was the most threatening whisper Patrick had ever heard and chilled him to the bone.

"I understand – sir," Patrick stood, placing his cap on his head as he did so. "I won't be taking up any more of your time. Nor shall I be thanking you for it, as you have told me nothing I did not already know. My wife regularly contributes some of my hard earned wages to Tammany. She maintains it does a power of good for the Irish community." Patrick turned and walked towards the door. "It's a pity she didn't accompany me here today, you might have taken a different view of our plight. I'm not very good with words, myself, sir."

"Blast you, man," the angry words halted Patrick in his tracks.

"My colleagues and I have put a lot of time and effort into cleaning up the reputation of this organization and I cannot let you walk out of my office having left such an accusation behind you. Do you not realise the difficult position I could find myself in if I was found to be in possession of so-called wrong information?"

Patrick slowly turned around, half afraid to do so, in the ten seconds of silence that followed the outburst. The face of the older man had intensified to such a vibrant red that the silver hair shone like a well-polished teapot.

"I beg your pardon, Mr. Whelan, I did not mean to offend you or anyone else here at Tammany. But I cannot face my brother's wife nor my own, for that matter, with another wasted day of searching."

"Then go straight to Mr. McGrother's employer, upon leaving this building and do not take his apparent ignorance for granted – and leave my name out of the conversation, if he will entertain you, that is. Now, if you will excuse me, I must attend to these papers. Good day to you, sir."

Patrick watched the older man return to his seat and pick up one of the sheets of paper, his eyes moving at an even pace across the page. The signal was not lost on him and, without a word of farewell, Patrick left the stuffy, warm office. Relieved to find the corridor empty, he took a deep breath of the cooler air. He contemplated whether or not to return to the barman who had pointed him in the direction of Tammany in the first place, but changed his mind as an image of the large, daunting frame came back to him.

Thomas's employer was much less threatening and with this in mind, Patrick set out towards Newspaper Row, were his brother-in-law's editor ran a small independent press. It was located down a side street, not too far from City Hall and the more prestigious newspapers of the day, such as The New York Times and New York Tribune.

CHAPTER TEN

Large damp spots were still visible on the freshly scrubbed flagstones, as Mary-Anne leaned against the wall of her new kitchen, surveying a good morning's work. She was exhausted but happy, the happiest she had ever been in her entire life. She was now the owner of a lodging house and tea-rooms. It would not be long before she had a thriving enterprise going, allowing her to take her place among the business community of Blackrock.

A shadow falling across the open doorway alerted Mary-Anne to someone's approach and she sprang across the kitchen floor like a cat on hot cinders, avoiding the flags bearing the dampest patches.

"Stay outside – the floor is wet."

A burst of male laughter revealed the identity of her visitor and Mary-Anne smiled warmly up into her father's eyes, as she stepped across the threshold into her back garden.

"That was a fair jig you danced across the kitchen floor, love. I take it you're pleased with the new flags?" James was relieved to see his normally sombre daughter in such good humour.

"Oh, Da, you are the best stonemason in Ireland and England. Did you know that? I've never seen such a level floor, not even in the big houses across the water – and I've been in some of their kitchens more times than I care to remember," Mary-Anne's face lost its brightness. "It's where I was made wait when I accompanied the Mistress to the homes of her wealthy friends. I was forced to drink endless cups of tea, while the cooks tried to pick my brains for a bit of gossip."

James smiled at the thought of anyone forcing his stubborn daughter to do something against her will. Not wanting her mood to darken, he gave her the good news her mother had sent with him.

"Your ma has been told of a young couple desiring a place to lodge when they pay a visit to Blackrock a week from now. Do you think you'll be open for business by then?"

The smile returned to Mary-Anne's face and she hugged her father tightly. "Yes. Yes, of course. Where did Ma hear about it? Does she know the family? Are they from the parish?"

"I don't know who they are or where they come from and that's not something that should be of concern to you, Mary-Anne. Business is business and as long as they can pay for their keep, that's all that matters. It was one of the neighbours mentioned it to your ma, I've forgotten who, but no doubt she will tell you herself," James watched as his daughter took off her apron and noticed how thin she had become. "Come up with me now to the house and have a bite to eat, you look half starved. George will be home from school by the time we get there and I daresay he's been missing you this past week."

Closing the door and turning the key in the lock, Mary-Anne felt an aching tiredness sweep over her. It had been a long week of cleaning and painting, with only her father's help in laying the floor. Her younger brother had not once offered his labour and Mary-Anne had been too stubborn to ask. Her mother and aunt did what they could but their efforts had not been up to the young woman's exacting standards.

Mary-Anne linked her father's arm as they strolled at a leisurely pace to the far end of town.

Neighbours greeted them with a warm smile as they passed by and both father and daughter knew that some would be itching to find out what kind of a transformation the tiny lodging house had undergone.

"I daresay you'll be running around like a headless chicken when you open your tea room, Mary-Anne, everyone knows what a grand wee cook you are. Sure the smell of your bread alone is enough to drag them all in from the street."

"I do hope so, Da. I've put every penny I had into this. I know I should have rented and kept my money in the bank, but with young Lord Devereux having to sell off some of the properties he inherited from his father, it was the perfect time to get a house at a good price. Do you not agree?" Mary-Anne was surprised at how much she wanted her father's approval.

"It was a very wise decision, love. You were blessed to have enough money saved to make such a purchase, and isn't it a grand thing to be able to say you own the roof that's over your head?" the pride was clearly discernible in James's voice.

"It is a grand thing, indeed. A very grand thing," Mary-Anne was fit to burst with happiness but she knew that the money she had accumulated had less to do with a blessing and more to do with a guilty conscience – and the threat of exposure.

"I was thinking of hiring a bit of help, just for the mornings. It will be difficult to keep up with everything when there are guests looking for breakfast and rooms to be cleaned and the day's meals to prepare. What do you think, yourself, Da?"

"Sure, your Ma will give you a helping hand, love. Hasn't she already told you as much?"

"I don't want to trouble her with more work, she's not as young as she thinks she is. No, I have someone in mind but I won't say who just yet, I want it to be a surprise."

"I suppose you look on me as an old man, so, Mary-Anne, judging by your remarks about your mother," James sighed.

"Ach, not at all, Da. Men don't age like women. If I'm to be truly honest about it, I would say that men become even more appealing the older they get."

James laughed out loud and shook his head, "Mary-Anne, you're more brazen than ever. I won't say who you take after, as I want to live long enough to enjoy my dinner this evening."

A mock scowl replaced Mary-Anne's smile but she inwardly delighted in being compared to her father's sister. Her Aunt Maggie was annoying and had a way of getting under Mary-Anne's skin, but she considered it a great compliment to be compared to the only woman who could come close to being her equal in an argument.

CHAPTER ELEVEN

With their children in bed, Patrick and Catherine sat each side of the large stove that warmed their small two bed-roomed apartment. A newspaper their son had brought home from work lay unopened on the table, their usual Friday night ritual of Catherine reading out to her husband abandoned by mutual consent.

"I'm short this week in my wages, love. I cannot afford to be arriving late at the quarry for much longer. I may lose my place there."

"Aye, it's a mercy indeed that you've not lost it already," Catherine replied. "I fear the time has come for us to inform the police about Thomas's absence."

A creaking floorboard turned their heads in the same direction. Young Tom was standing in the doorway of the bedroom he shared with his sisters.

"Well, son? Are you not able to sleep?"

"No, Da. I'm not, but I have something from Mr. McIntyre to give to you and I had to wait until the girls were asleep before I could do so. He said I was not to let anyone else know about it but I think it's alright for Ma to see this."

Tom opened his clenched fist to reveal a small white conch shell. It was attached to a thick cotton thread and at the sight of it both of his parents jumped to their feet.

"I knew what it was the minute he gave it me," said Tom.

"Gave it *to* me, Tom," his mother corrected him automatically, out of habit, as she continued to stare at his hand.

"You know what this means, don't you, Catherine? Thomas must be in trouble but at least he's alive," Patrick answered his own question.

"Is there a tiny note from him hidden inside the shell, Tom? Have a look."

The boy shook his head, "No, Ma. I've already poked and poked; there's nothing in there. Mr. McIntyre told me I'm not to be fretting over Uncle Thomas and that he has news of him for Da."

Catherine took the shell from his hand and patted her son on the back. "Off to bed with you, now. You've an early start in the morning and won't be fit for a decent day's work if you don't get your sleep." She held up her hand, waving the shell in front of Tom, "This is a good sign. Your uncle is well and he wants us to know it. Sure, you know how cautious he must be about his comings and goings on many of his assignments."

"Your ma is right, Tom. Away with you to your bed, son, and try not to dwell too much on this or you'll not get a wink of sleep. I'll be going with you to your work in the morning to hear what news Mr. McIntyre has."

As soon as the bedroom door closed Catherine ran into her husband's arms, clutching the tiny shell to her heart.

"He's in terrible trouble, Patrick. Our Thomas is either too weak or in too much danger to write to us – he might even be dead by now. Oh, what are we to do? How can we give such news to poor Lily?"

They stood embracing for a long time. James McGrother had given a shell each to Thomas and Catherine, as a reminder of their roots, before they left for America. The tiny mementos had come from a string of shells that Catherine, as a small child, had collected for her father at a time when he was gravely ill. To anyone outside the family they would seem worthless and childish but to the McGrothers they had a very special meaning.

Patrick knew that if he was to open the top button on his wife's blouse he would find a silver chain with two small items attached to it. When the family had emigrated from Ireland Catherine was so nervous of crossing the wide expanse of the Atlantic, from Liverpool to New York, that Patrick bought her a Saint Christopher medal – the patron saint of travellers – for the journey. She had worn it ever since.

Looped onto the chain beside the medal hung a tiny white conch shell.

"Let's be getting to bed, love. I daresay it will be good news Mr. McIntyre has for us," but Patrick was more worried than he cared to admit.

******

"Mr. Gallagher, good morning to you."

Patrick took the outstretched hand and inwardly smiled at how often his name had been prefixed by *'Mister'* over the past few weeks. Most of his day would normally be spent answering to the call of 'Gallagher' at work or 'Da' at home. His wife and Lily along with some neighbours and friends called him by his first name, so the title 'Mr. Gallagher' made it sound as if another man was being addressed.

Thomas's editor and owner of the newspaper was a down to earth man who wore a handlebar moustache that tapered to the thinnest waxed points Patrick had ever seen. It was distracting to look at so he turned his head towards the glazed panels surrounding them, giving a full view of the workshop. Patrick had the uncomfortable feeling of being suspended in a glass box, even the noise was muted somewhat. He could see why his son loved the place, with its small work force and friendly atmosphere.

As his eyes skimmed quickly over the workshop the sight of an older man showing a younger one how to take a piece of machinery apart brought a smile to his face.

"Your son is a fast learner and a diligent worker, Mr. Gallagher. A fine young man, you should be proud."

Patrick was aware of the other man looking over his shoulder at the same scene and turned around, still smiling.

"Oh, I am and so is his mother, even more so. Do you have children, Mr. McIntyre?"

"I do, five daughters and not a son among them?"

"And do you have a brother or a sister, yourself?"

In spite of thinking this an unusual question Mr. McIntyre tweaked both points of his moustache and answered, "One of each still living, by the grace of God."

"So you can appreciate the pain my wife is going through at the loss of her brother, can you not?" Patrick held out a fist and opened it to reveal the tiny shell.

"Please, sit down, Patrick. May I call you that? And you must call me William. I think we've been in each other's company enough times now to dispense with the formalities, eh?"

Patrick nodded as he took his seat, "I wasted a morning at Tammany when I should have been at my work. The advice I got was to come here. Now why do you think I was told that?"

"I see," William replied, "Who was it that sent you?"

"Well now, I was told most definitely not to bring his name up in conversation with you. Does that answer your question?"

"It does, Patrick. It does indeed. I had asked for assistance from Tammany as soon as it was apparent that Thomas was in trouble. I'm in no way surprised at the response. Political sensitivities are given more consideration than an individual's needs in cases such as this. Thomas had been to Tammany, to see Mr. Whelan, a week before he left New York."

"That shell was either sent by Thomas or taken from him," Patrick looked straight into the other man's eyes, "I suspect a message of some sort came with it."

"And you would be correct in your thinking, Patrick," as he spoke, William took a small wooden box from a drawer at the side of his desk.

He opened it to reveal a letter and held the box out to Patrick, who shook his head, explaining, "I'm not much of a reader at the best of times."

"I understand," William replied, "I can tell you for a certainty this is from Thomas, although he has not signed it. I would know his neat hand anywhere."

Mr. McIntyre went on to inform Patrick that Thomas was with a group of men working a coal mine in Pennsylvania. He had gone there because of a letter he had received from his father, asking if he could track down a young man who had not been heard from in over a year.

"I remember Thomas speaking of such a letter some months ago. I know this young man and his family, they would be neighbours of the McGrothers.

"You understand this must remain strictly between the two of us. Not even a whisper to your wife or to Lily. Do I have your word on that, Patrick?"

"You do, on my mother's grave, but why must we be so secretive? Men are often slow about sending word home."

"Thomas was reluctant to speak of the circumstances surrounding this young man's disappearance. Have you ever heard tell of the notorious runner, Heartless Hannigan and his scandalous treatment of those escaping the famine in Ireland, back in the '40's?" asked William.

"Do you mean the Irishman who rowed out to board the coffin ships quarantined in the bay, to take advantage of his own people?"

"What do you know of Hannigan, Patrick?"

"I know that he spoke to those poor unfortunates in their own tongue to gain their trust, promising food and shelter to any he thought might survive the fever, and then sold them off to the highest bidder? What has he got to do with this? Sure, didn't he drown in a drunken stupor, and good enough for him, I say."

"He most definitely did not drown and Thomas discovered that fact almost as soon as he began his search for this young man. Heartless Hannigan is alive and well and up to his old tricks again – only this time he's not selling off his victims." William squirmed, as if a bad taste had come into his mouth, "No, he's keeping them for himself, as slaves."

Patrick made to spit on the ground, then realised he was indoors. He swallowed to alleviate the sting of bile in his throat and was relieved to see the older man pour some whiskey into two small tumblers.

"I think we both have need of this," William swallowed his in one gulp, then refilled his glass.

Patrick drank his just as fast but refused a second, reminding himself that he had almost a day's work ahead.

"How old do you think Hannigan might be now, William?"

"Must be in his early sixties. He was a young man, in his twenties I would say, when he was a runner but times were hard then and people did whatever it took to survive under the circumstances. Had you arrived here forty years ago you would have had a very different reception, Patrick. Hannigan came off one of those coffin ships after losing his mother and younger brother on the journey over."

"Are you expecting me to feel sorry for him?" Patrick interrupted.

"Not at all, there's no excuse for what he did. I'm telling you what may have driven him to such unscrupulous acts. He boarded that ship with the only family he had left in the world. Apparently, his father and sisters died from starvation and fever, so his mother took the landlord's offer of paid passage to America. He was the only one of his family that did not get sick on that ship. Some say it was the reason he became a runner, tempting faith to see if he could join his family in the grave."

"I doubt very much that was his reason. More as like, he felt the fever could not touch him and he had no fear of it," Patrick replied in disgust.

"Well, whatever drove him to do such evil deeds is still at work in him today and from what Thomas has written, Hannigan is even more heartless than he ever was and dangerous with it. He goes by the name of Hartigan nowadays. In the past, before Tammany cleared itself of corruption, Hannigan had regular business deals with certain members that even extended to the law. It still remains a sensitive topic, even today."

"Did nobody approach the police about this? Not even the family back in Ireland?" asked Patrick.

"They did, indeed, but got the same response as Thomas. Do you have any suggestions as to how we can get your brother-in-law out of this mess?"

The whole time Mr. McIntyre was speaking, a plan had been struggling to form in the young man's head.

"I must be truthful with you, William, the biggest obstacle to me reaching Thomas is my work. I can take leave of absence for one week, but it will be without a wage and I have little savings as such to keep my rent paid and my family fed. If I were to take any more time from my work, I would lose my position at the quarry. There's a long list of names ready to take my place, should it become available. Can we not approach the police, surely the note is enough proof that a crime has been committed?"

"That could very well put Thomas in more danger than he is in already. No, you are his only hope, Patrick," as William was speaking, he removed a wad of money from his inside pocket and placed it on the table. "Thomas made arrangements to provide for his family if he did not return. You would consider yourself part of his family, would you not?"

Patrick was stunned. The realization that Thomas had voluntarily put himself in a situation that he knew to be so dangerous had a strange effect on him. He was angry that a man who always sat on the fence and saw both sides of every conflict, should decide to become an activist without telling him. At the same time a new admiration for Thomas began to grow in Patrick's heart.

"I made a promise to my wife before we left Ireland that I would not become involved in anything that could bring trouble to our door," Patrick's voice was so low, William thought he may have been thinking out loud.

In the silence that followed, the sound of men calling to each other over the rhythm of machinery filled the small room.

"Is your wife not desperate to have her brother back safely with his family? Thomas must trust you to act discreetly or he would never have sent this message. The agreement we made before he left was that I should inform you, and only you, should help be needed. And that your family be provided for," William pointed to the money on the desk.

Patrick stood up, unable to shake the feeling that a price had just been put upon his loyalty. "I'll go now and inform my overseer that I'll be taking leave of absence," he peeled away half the notes from the wad of money, leaving the rest back on the table, "You had best hold onto that until I bring Thomas back with me. He will have need of it himself, no doubt."

"Please Patrick, take the rest of the money with you. You can tell Lily and your wife that Thomas left it in case his absence became overly long."

"I have enough for the journey, Mr. McIntyre," Patrick had reverted to formality, "And I shall give some to Lily and let her know there's more here if she needs it."

Having walked towards one of the windows, Patrick looked down at his son's figure, bent low over a printing machine in the workshop below. "Judging from what Thomas has written, I should not be gone much more than a week. Young Tom will be the man of the house in my absence. Between his earnings and my savings the family can manage, my Catherine is very good with money, or the lack of it." Patrick swung round to face the older man, "Good day to you, sir. I'm very much obliged for your concern."

William firmly shook the hand extended towards him and knew by the set look on Patrick's face that it would be useless to argue over the money. Watching him leave the office, he silently resolved to include a bonus in Tom's wage that week.

CHAPTER TWELVE

Although the spring weather had warmed up during the daytime, the night was a different matter. As soon as the sun had set the chill crept in, searching out the men's bones. It had been too dangerous to build a fire, so huddling together was the only source of heat available to the three hungry men, sheltering under a bush.

"Let me see your eye, Petey. The cloud is after breaking and there's a grand full moon in the sky," said Thomas.

"Never mind my eye, have a look at Dinny's foot. Has the swelling gone down at all?"

Thomas pulled up the tattered end of a trouser leg belonging to their elderly companion, to expose an ankle so swollen and black, it looked ready to explode. Even in the dim light, the men could see the extent of the injury.

"Dinny. Wake up Dinny. It's too cold to sleep. Come on, man, keep the blood flowing through your veins," Thomas rubbed the limp arms.

There was no warming up the old man, who remained half sitting, half lying, against the tangled branches of their crude shelter. Thomas leaned in to the weathered face and placed the back of his hand close to where Dinny's mouth was lost in a wiry grey beard.

"I think he's dead, Petey. I can't feel his breath."

Both men made the sign of the cross, an automatic response even for Thomas who claimed to be an unbeliever.

"Are you sure he's gone? He's a very deep sleeper, Thomas. Sure, wasn't he always getting a beating back at the mine, for being missing from the morning line-up? No matter how many times I tried to pull him from his bunk it was only the lash of a whip that stirred him."

Having checked once more for a heartbeat and a pulse in the old man's neck, Thomas shook his head slowly as he pulled Dinny's tattered hat down over his eyes.

"He was an old man, Petey, I reckon his heart just gave out. All we can do for him now, is give him a decent burial." Thomas stood and stretched his aching legs, "Stand up and help me carry him to a nice resting place before the clouds blot out the light again."

Thomas glanced around the scrubland as he helped his young friend rise shakily to his feet. A piece of high ground a short distance away caught his eye and he pointed it out to Petey. The dead man's weight seemed to have doubled and Thomas wondered how they had managed to carry him over the rugged terrain when he had broken his ankle. Dinny had asked them to leave him behind but the men had refused to abandon their friend.

Having spent a good hour gathering enough rocks to cover their old companion as best they could, Thomas and Petey stood at each end of the long narrow mound. They knew that wild animals would dig him out and the buzzards would finish off whatever was left, but they would be long gone by then and spared the reminders of what their own fate might be.

Petey elected to say a prayer, knowing how Thomas felt about religion of any sort.

"I don't know whether he was a Catholic or not, do you?" Petey realised, having said a decade of the Rosary over the grave.

"I reckon he was. Sure, wasn't he born in Clare? Aren't they all mostly Catholic there? Especially the ones that got evicted."

"I suppose you're right, Thomas. It's a great pity we don't know of his family but he never spoke of them – only that they were forced out of their home to join the *'throngs of walking skeletons'* as Dinny used to say. He was a peculiar old man all the same, wasn't he?"

"He was, Petey. He was, indeed."

"Did you know he was in the Irish Brigade, Thomas? He once told me he fought at Gettysburg?"

"I never knew that? Well, we've buried him in a fitting place so, Petey. Gettysburg isn't a million miles from here.

Thomas had met plenty of men like Dinny, itinerant workers good with a pick and shovel, traveling to wherever there was work to be had. Many had arrived from the ports of Ireland and England on 'coffin' ships and for a great number of men, the army provided a bed, food and a wage. Indeed, Irishmen had served on both sides of the Civil War.

As the moon disappeared behind a cloud Thomas shivered, "We should continue our journey through the night to keep ourselves from getting chilled. What do you say?"

Petey assured Thomas that he wasn't in the least bit weary and would prefer to be walking, rather than lying awake shivering. Retrieving his hat from a nearby rock, he asked, "How shall we know which direction to take? We cannot see the stars and I doubt those clouds are going to clear before morning."

"The breeze has been against our faces all day and coming from the east, where our destination lies. We must continue to face into the wind," Thomas was already striding ahead.

There was a mutual silence between the men as they walked, their emotions changing with every few steps. It had been hard going carrying Dinny, slowing them down in their efforts to put distance between themselves and the place that had almost been the death of them. Now they were covering three times as much ground, the cold night air spurring them on in an effort to keep warm.

"As much as it makes finding our way difficult, those dense clouds covering the stars are keeping a bit of heat in, Petey."

"Even so, we're making great progress without . . ." the younger man's voice trailed off.

"Poor old Dinny. He was worked almost to death before we left that place," said Thomas.

Their journey continued in silence as each man considered his own fate and tried to prepare himself for what might lie ahead.

"Is that the lights of a house I can see, or do my eyes play tricks on me, Thomas?"

"I think we might be approaching the outskirts of the town. We should make our way towards those trees over yonder and wait until the evening draws in again before going any further. What do you say, Petey?"

The young man looked at the ever lightening dawn sky and agreed with Thomas, "Do you think your friend will have reached the town yet?"

"Oh, that I do not doubt, Petey, not for one minute. If my letter reached its intended destination, he will have come. I'm certain of it."

Thomas patted his young companion on the back, "We must finish what we've started now, if we are to have any chance of seeing our families again. Or do you think it safer we go our separate ways? I would not like to think I have forced you into returning to Ireland."

"Wild horses could not drag me from your side, Thomas. When you spoke of my mother, my one thought was to get back to her. I pray it won't be too long until I complete the journey – if I complete it, that is. When I left home to seek adventure in America I was sure that my absence would hardly be noticed. After all, I'm the youngest of four sons."

"The youngest has a special place in a mother's heart, Petey. As time goes by and a woman accepts that her child-bearing years have come to an end, her love towards her youngest one changes."

"How do you know these things? You're a strange kettle of fish altogether, Thomas."

"It was my father told me that. He's a very observant man and I have him to thank for my social conscience."

"And was it him gave you such a strange way of speaking. I have difficulty understanding your words at times, Thomas."

A fit of laughter from his companion lifted Petey's spirits, he liked it when others found what he said amusing. Being humorous had gotten the young man out of many a scrape.

"I cannot blame my father for that. No, it was books that gave me my peculiar turn of phrase. You should learn to read, Petey, books can bring the world to your door without you ever having to step foot on board a vessel."

"I wish I had known that before leaving home, so. It would have saved me a pile of trouble."

Thomas laughed again and remarked that should Petey ever learn to read and write, he would have enough to fill a book of his own about his adventures in America. The sound of hens clucking told them there would be raw eggs for breakfast and they may even have a chance to steal a little milk from the cow they could hear lowing in the barn.

"Come along, Petey, let's get some sustenance before the family rises to tend their animals. It will take the edge off our hunger while we catch up on our sleep. With any luck, we shall have a hot meal this evening, or tomorrow at the latest."

CHAPTER THIRTEEN

Jamie squinted as early morning rays of sunshine bounced off the white, newly painted façade of his sister's lodging house. Pulling the peak of his cap down to meet his eyebrows, the young man quickened his step, cursing himself for not walking on the other side of the street. It irritated him that Mary-Anne had come home to flaunt her wealth in front of the whole parish.

"Hold your horses, Jamie McGrother."

His sister's voice halted him in his tracks, an automatic response from his childhood.

'Damn and blast her,' the phrase repeated itself in his head as Jamie turned on his heel.

"What's your hurry, *boy*?" the word being emphasized for effect.

"Stop calling me that, Mary-Anne. You're only nine years older than me. What is it you want?"

"Who says I want anything? I've managed without any help from you up to now. I spoke with your wife after Mass on Sunday and was wondering if she had mentioned my offer to you," Mary-Anne waved at one of her neighbours as she spoke.

"I know you did and her answer is no. I am well able to provide for the both of us. Now, if you'll excuse me, I've a busy day ahead," Jamie turned and walked away.

It was just as Mary-Anne had expected. Annie's eyes had lit up at the offer of work from her sister-in-law but they didn't stay bright for long, when she spotted her young husband glaring at her through the crowd outside the church. *"I shall have to discuss it with Jamie before giving you my answer,"* was Annie's reply. Mary-Anne knew what his response would be.

"You're a stubborn mule, Jamie McGrother. Always have been and it will be to your detriment, mark my words," Mary-Anne shouted after him.

Jamie fumed his way to the end of the street, his sister's words clanging in his ears like a ship's bell in the fog. It wasn't long before he arrived at the little two-roomed cottage where he knew his young wife would have breakfast waiting for him. The anticipation of seeing her smiling face and the smell of freshly baked bread softened his anger and lightened his step.

As soon as she heard the door open, Annie was in his arms, the novelty of being a fisherman's wife still fresh. Her father and brothers were farm labourers, who rose at cockcrow to spend their working day in the fields. Jamie did most of his work by night and his young wife was not yet comfortable spending so many dark, silent hours alone.

On those nights when the wind picked up, whistling through any gaps it found in the old thatched roof, Annie would sit up in bed worrying and praying for her husband's safe return. At times she invited her younger sister to spend the night, which kept her mind occupied and fearful thoughts at bay. Before she married Jamie, the girls had shared the same bed. To Annie, the light snoring of her sister still felt more natural than the sound of a man sleeping by her side.

Jamie could feel the heat coming from his wife as she buried herself in his arms. The pleasure of a good night's fishing had not been totally diminished by the encounter with his sister and it only served to heighten the emotions that Annie could still awaken in him. After six months of marriage, Jamie had expected those feelings to lessen, as he assumed they did for other married men. He could tell that Annie felt the same way, in spite of her putting on the air of a well settled wife when in the company of others.

"Let me get myself washed and sweet-smelling for you, love," laughed Jamie.

He was pleased to see the only other door in the small house lying open, a good sign that their bed was empty.

"Did your sister not keep you company last night, Annie?" Jamie tried to sound blasé as he washed in the bowl of hot water his wife had placed on the kitchen table.

"I didn't ask her to. I'll just have to get used to being a fisherman's wife and that's that. I slept like a baby," her reply echoing his matter-of-fact tone.

Annie took a few steps back to lean against the closed front door of the cottage. She loved to watch the muscles flex in her husband's arms as he washed away the sweat of his labouring.

"Come and scrub my back, Annie, instead of standing behind me admiring the view?"

"What a cheek, Jamie McGrother! Do you think that's all I have to do?" was her indignant reply.

Jamie spun round to face his wife and the look in his eyes melted her heart. Taking the wet cloth from his hand, she reprimanded him for dripping water all over her clean floor. She was still berating him as he lifted her off her feet and carried her into the bedroom.

Their love-making was still as intense as in the first few days of their marriage and Annie wondered if every wife felt as she did. When she finally plucked up the courage to ask her mother about it the answer she got was to enjoy it while it lasted.

"Jamie, are you asleep?"

There was a soft groan, "Do you have to whisper so loudly, Annie?"

"Do you think it a sin that we behave so.... so.... do you know what I'm trying to say?"

Jamie turned on his side, putting his face close to Annie's.

"And if I say *yes*, are you going to tell it in confession?" he kissed the tip of her nose. "Because I certainly will not. Now let me get some decent sleep. Do you not have a hundred chores waiting for you, or so you are always telling me?"

"Promise me you won't discuss this with anyone, Jamie?"

"Annie, you are the one who started this. Promise me the same thing."

A pang of guilt stabbed briefly at the young wife as she recalled the conversation with her mother. "Oh for goodness sake, I have more to be doing than talking nonsense at this hour of the morning," she scolded, jumping out of the warm bed.

The wail of a crying infant sounded through the wall behind their bed and Annie sighed.

"As soon as we have one of those, we'll forget about all that *sinning* we've been getting up to," she said.

Jamie drowsily watched his wife as she dressed and knew he would always have the same longing for her, even after the arrival of a baby.

"I suppose you're right," came his sleepy reply.

The back door to Mary-Anne's newly painted lodging house lay wide open, so Annie loudly announced her arrival as she walked into the well-scrubbed kitchen.

"Why must you shout like a street hawker? I'm not deaf, Annie," Mary-Anne scolded as she came in from the hallway.

"I beg your pardon, Ma'am. I thought you were upstairs," Annie used the title her sister-in-law had requested.

"There's no need for the formalities when we are alone, my dear. When we are in the company of guests you can call me Ma'am, but most of the time you will be in the kitchen and unlikely to meet any of my lodgers."

"Yes, Mary-Anne. Do you want me to prepare the vegetables like I did yesterday?"

"That would be very helpful, Annie. I can see you are a quick learner. I hope you're going to tell that sour husband of yours what you are doing, before he finds out from someone else."

"I will indeed but I must time it well. And he's not sour," Annie turned towards the stove, "*At least not with me,*" she whispered to herself.

"Well, I shall leave you to get on with your work. You'll need to hurry back as soon as you finish, before Jamie wakes up to an empty house," Mary-Anne picked up a neatly folded pile of bedlinen to take upstairs. "I asked him this morning about you coming to work for me and he stormed off in a temper."

Annie chopped a head of cabbage into a large pot that held a joint of bacon. She had just finished preparing some biscuit dough when Mary-Anne came back into the kitchen.

"Did you not hear that knock on the front door, Annie?"

"I heard the knock but I cannot be seen here yet, Mary-Anne. Not until I've told Jamie about it. The biscuits are almost ready for the oven and the bacon and cabbage are coming to the boil, so I'd best be on my way."

"Thank you, Annie. No, I suppose you're right to be cautious, at least until you tell Jamie about your work here." Mary-Anne took some coins from her pocket, "I would rather pay you by the day, so here is our agreed sum. Shall I see you tomorrow?"

As Annie bade farewell she assured her sister-in-law that she would be standing in the same spot every morning except Sunday and Jamie would be aware of that fact by the end of the week.

"She's a feisty one, no doubt about it," Mary-Anne said aloud to the empty kitchen. "Our Jamie has met his match in her."

The telegram that had been delivered was still in her hand and she unfolded it to read the name once more. It wasn't a familiar one and Mary-Anne wondered how the man had managed to find out about her lodging house but she was not going to spend too long thinking on it. Her first guests, a young couple from Cavan, would be rising soon and looking for breakfast.

"I think I'll give them an extra egg this morning. They won't be used to the sea air, and its saltiness has a strange way of increasing the appetite of those not accustomed to it," Mary-Anne was in a generous mood, her first week as a landlady having started off so well.

CHAPTER FOURTEEN

The town was large enough to have a good mix of saloons, lodging houses and provision stores, all of which attracted a wide variety of people. Thomas was pleased to find plenty of hard living, hard working men, looking similar to themselves. It would be easy to blend into the crowd while they searched for one man in particular.

Being unfamiliar with the area, Thomas had relied on his keen powers of observation and sharp memory to record the main towns that surrounded the mine where he had been held captive. A sign over the general store told him they had arrived in the same town that he had mentioned in his message to his employer, Mr. McIntyre. Unfortunately, Thomas had no way of knowing with certainty that his letter had been delivered safely and in good time.

"Why are we entering the church, Thomas? Have you found your faith again?"

"No, Petey, I most definitely have not, but I thought you might have need of a prayer yourself – or am I wrong in my assumption."

The young man looked around the interior of the simple wooden building. Long, roughly hewn benches, with no similarity whatsoever to the highly polished pews found in most churches, lined each side of a short aisle. Petey could see why its door had no lock, there wasn't even a brass candlestick to be seen.

"It doesn't look like a Catholic church, Thomas. I don't think we should stay here. I'll do my praying when I get to a proper house of God."

"From what I can see, Petey, this is the only house of God we are going to find in this town,"

Thomas pointed to the darkest area of the church, "We should take a seat over there."

"Who are we waiting for?"

"Well, I can tell you that it's not a man of God. Most definitely not. You'll have to wait and see, Petey. The reason I cannot give you a name is because we are still not out of danger of being captured and what you do not know, you cannot tell. It's not a matter of trust but of caution."

"I think I'll chance a quick prayer while we're here, so. I'll pray that your friend finds us and leads us all to safety. I'm sure God won't mind if it's only a quick one. What do you think, Thomas?"

"You do that and I'll keep a lookout, in case your prayer is answered before you get to the end of it."

As one man knelt in prayer, the other scanned the shadows. It was Dinny who told Thomas about the plain little church where he had offered up a rare supplication on an empty stomach, having lost all his money gambling in one of the town's saloons. When Thomas asked if his prayer had been answered, Dinny said he hoped not. *'If the angel of mercy that was sent to me came from God, then the world is in a heap of trouble,'* Thomas smiled as he recalled Dinny's words. The following day a large sum of money was loaned to him by no other than Hannigan himself – or Hartigan, as Dinny called him. Unable to resist the urge to redeem some of his own lost fortune, he gambled away every cent of what he had borrowed and found himself owing a debt that had been impossible to pay.

The old man's story had confirmed Thomas's suspicion that Hannigan was in league with at least one of the town's saloons, but when Dinny revealed that Hannigan was the owner of the establishment it all made sense to Thomas. Everything he had learned from his investigation into Petey's disappearance pointed to one particular saloon and Thomas had allowed himself to become beholden to one of Hannigan's henchmen, in order to test out his findings.

It wasn't long before he too, like Dinny, had gambled away every last cent loaned to him and Thomas found himself being hauled in front of the local sheriff. He was given the choice of prison or working to pay off his debt. Thomas chose to work and, in spite of his dire circumstances, it was a great relief to find that Petey was among the group of men that had been tricked into working for Hannigan to repay a debt.

The low hum of a whispered chant broke into Thomas's ruminating.

"Say a Rosary, Petey, we might need it."

"I am, Thomas. I'm saying a decade," came a whispered reply.

"The whole Rosary, Petey."

"Things must be worse than I thought. A whole Rosary it is, so."

Thomas patted his young friend on the shoulder and smiled at the low, rhythmic muttering that followed. In spite of being an unbeliever, the sound of a prayerful chant was a comforting reminder of his childhood and the family in Ireland. He was determined to see them again, some day, and the thought of Lily being widowed with a young child to rear, increased the adrenaline that had been diminishing in the relative safety of his surroundings.

A creaking of wood echoing in the darkness sent Thomas's pulse racing. Petey, deep in prayer, heard nothing and didn't even notice his companion inch closer to him. A man's form emerged from the shadows and although Thomas knew by the shape and walk it was the person he had been waiting for, he was not prepared to take any chances.

In spite of being positioned a small distance from the town, the sound of men shouting and women laughing reached into the quiet darkness of the church and Thomas realised the door had been left open. He knew if the man standing in the shadows had meant them any harm he would have closed it behind him. A familiar whistle brought a smile to Thomas's face.

"Over here, Patrick."

Abandoning his prayers, Petey watched as the figure of a man drew close and he tried to make out the face, half hidden under a wide brimmed hat. A list of all the Patricks he knew began to form in his head.

Thomas ran forward and embraced his brother-in-law, relief flooding through him. Pulling him back to where Petey stood, he laughed as a wide grin replaced the anxious look on the young man's face.

"I take it you remember Patrick Gallagher?"

"Remember? How could I forget," Petey grasped Patrick's hand. "This will be the second time you've come to my rescue. Did you know, Thomas, that your brother-in-law saved me from drowning and then taught me to swim so it wouldn't happen again?"

"I did indeed, Petey. Sure didn't the whole of county Louth hear about it?" laughed Thomas.

"And rightly so," Petey was still shaking Patrick's hand.

"Well, we are not out of the water, yet. I have a room nearby and I've told the landlady you will be joining me. She has a hot meal on the stove for us but we must wait until the stage gets here as she thinks I'm to meet you off it." Patrick looked in the direction of the open door, "Petey, go and keep watch for it, there's a good man. Tell us as soon as it passes by."

"I have some clothes for ye," Patrick sniffed his brother-in-law's jacket. "And judging by the smell of what you're wearing, it's a good thing, too."

Thomas rummaged through the bundle and quickly changed his clothes, while Patrick gave him news of the family. They were interrupted by Petey informing them of the stagecoach's arrival.

"Change out of those rags you're wearing and make yourself presentable, Petey," Patrick handed over a small sack, "When we get to our lodgings you can wash yourselves at the pump before you eat. It's not only your clothes that are stinking. How did you manage to get through the town without drawing attention to yourselves?"

"We blended in quite nicely with the local drunks and everyone else gave us a wide berth," Thomas laughed, "Mind you, with our Petey here looking so handsome and dandy in his new attire, we shall probably attract a swarm of young ladies as soon as we leave the premises – body odour or not."

"Until they get close enough to see my poor eye, Thomas. That will soon send them running. What shall I say about it, should anyone ask?" Petey added.

"There's many a young man in this town sporting a black eye from what I've seen," Patrick replied. "I don't think it will raise too many questions but keep your hat pulled down low while we are in the streets."

"When did you get here, Patrick?" asked Thomas.

"Four days ago. I'm sure everyone thinks I'm a very devout man with the amount of visits I've been paying to this church since I got here. I was beginning to think your plan had gone wrong, Thomas. The lodging house I'm taking you to is only a short walk from here. It's owned by a Dublin woman. I don't think you could throw a stone in this town without hitting an Irish person."

In spite of their lodgings being so close, the men found it difficult to take that first step away from the safety of their refuge. The door of the small wooden church didn't quite face the dusty road leading into the town and a group of shrubs, someone's attempt at making a garden, gave them a degree of cover as they left the building.

Thomas was last to leave, Patrick having gone first, and while awaiting his turn he glanced at a large wooden cross hanging on the wall opposite the doorway. It was devoid of the tortured figure that had saddened Thomas so much as a child. The lack of statues or icons of devotion appealed to him and made the little church seem even more sacrosanct than any grand cathedral he had ever set foot in. It had a strange effect on a man who had given up on religion and Thomas found himself saying a quick prayer. At the sound of a low whistle from Patrick, he took a deep breath

and, bracing himself for trouble, stepped into the
night.

CHAPTER FIFTEEN

Paddy Mac was shorthanded and when that happened on a busy night everyone knew to order two drinks at a time, which made him work twice as hard with each serving. Jamie's fingers had a tight grip on the handles of four glass tankards. Carefully, he manoeuvred through a thirsty crowd that lined the bar three men deep.

"I still cannot believe that Packie Sullivan has a child. He's four years younger than myself." Jamie handed over two of the tankards to his father before taking his seat, "One of those drinks is on him and the other is on me, Da."

Money had been scarce for his parents of late, as Maggie's health had taken a turn for the worse and they had been paying for treatments to alleviate the constant pain in her legs. In spite of this, Jamie's father refused to accept any financial help from him and the fish he dropped in to his mother was the only bit of support he was allowed to give.

James nodded at his son then called across the noisy room to thank the new father, raising his tankard in salute.

"It won't be long before I'm here celebrating another grandchild myself, I daresay," he gave a sideways glance before taking a mouthful of beer.

"Now you're sounding like Ma," Jamie laughed, "You'll be the first one I tell the good news to, as soon as I hear it myself. I shall make sure Annie keeps it a secret from the family until you've heard it first."

"I'm very honoured you feel that way but your efforts to conceal news of that nature will be in vain, son – sure your Ma and your Aunt Maggie will be aware of Annie's condition well before she knows it herself."

"Well, if they take you into their confidence, you must be sure to tell me, so I can pass on the good news to my wife," Jamie would not have been surprised should it turn out that way.

"Speaking of confiding, I've been a bit concerned about something of late, do you think we could take the boat out tomorrow after Mass?" James saw a frown cross his son's face. "Now don't go fretting over it. It's nothing of a serious nature, I just want a quiet word and you know how I love to get out in the bay, sure any excuse will do."

"Is it fatherly advice you're wanting to give me, Da?"

"Something of that nature," James replied.

The following afternoon father and son met up at the southernmost end of Blackrock's beach, where Jamie kept his boat. Some of the other fishermen in the village were already in their vessels, providing short trips along the shoreline for day trippers and holidaymakers. It was a good way to supplement their income while still adhering to the generally accepted rule of not working on a Sunday. Greetings were shouted from boat to boat until the two McGrother men found themselves a good distance out in the bay.

"When was the last time ye won a game, son?" James had thrown a line into the water, a ragworm dangling on its end.

"A game of what, Da? Hurling?"

"Aye, hurling. I reckon it's been a long time, a good six months or more."

Being captain, Jamie was immediately on the defensive, "Sure half the team are wed now, Da, and working all the hours God sends - the other half are too busy trying to catch a woman, to turn up for the training."

"I reckon ye should change your method of training, so," a fish pulled on James's line as he spoke. "Maybe ye should be using your camáns to pick up a sliotar, instead of marching around with them thrown across your shoulders.

Jamie had been lying on his back, hands behind his head, sleepy and content under the warm afternoon sun. His body immediately tensed at his father's words. Preparing himself for the argument that was about to follow, the young man sat up, pulling the peak of his cap low in an attempt to hide the grim expression set on his face.

James kept his eye on the line as it dragged erratically through the water, "Well? Have you nothing to say to me on the matter?"

"Are you not going to pull that line in, before you lose the fish altogether. It looks to be a fine catch," Jamie ignored his father's question, hoping the struggling fish would divert his attention.

With a sudden hard yank on the line, James landed a good sized mullet in the boat between them. Both men watched as it flapped about, still putting up a good fight, struggling to break free and make its way back into the water. Jamie was taken by surprise when his father began to unlace one of his boots.

"What are you doing? You're not thinking of throwing yourself in are you, Da? Sure, you know I can swim. I'll just fish you back out again," Jamie was speaking in jest but his father's silence and strange behaviour was beginning to worry him.

Quick as a flash, James brought the heel of his heavy boot down onto the fish's head. It was done with such speed and force as to send his son scrambling backwards, setting the boat rocking in the calm water. He rained down so many continuous blows all over the body of his catch that it was only fit for bait by the time he had finished. The two men stared in silence at the mess of flesh, bone and guts lying between them.

"Well, I've never seen a fish gutted like that before. You've ruined what could have been a fine meal, Da."

James dangled his boot in the water, cleansing it of macerated flesh. "Have you ever seen a man after a beating such as that, son?"

"Why would you ask such a question? I have not, and would never want to." Jamie picked up his oars, "I think we should be getting back. I promised Annie I would not delay too long."

"Put the oars down and listen to what I have to say."

Not since his teenage years had Jamie heard his father use such a harsh tone of voice with him. It had the immediate effect of making him drop the oars and pull his cap even further down over his face.

"Take your cap off and let me look you in the eye, son. Why do you think I tried to discourage you from pursuing that young wife of yours?"

"Oh, no. Not that again. I thought we had come to an agreement about that. Sure, aren't you happy she has turned out to be such a fine daughter to you? Can you not be satisfied that I chose a good woman for a wife?"

"I once saw a man cry his heart out over the body of his son, beaten to death, much like that fish, Jamie."

James went on to give an account of the involvement of his old friend, Michael Kiernan, in the fight for independence and how it eventually led to the death of his son at the hands of a crazed policeman.

"He took his own life not long after that. I had to collect his body and arrange his funeral. You were only a young child at the time, so you won't remember too much about it. I even lied to a priest, telling him Michael had died by accidentally shooting himself, so that he could be buried with his son in sacred ground."

Jamie nodded, "I remember his wife, Brigid, when she came home to visit her son's grave. She brought us presents from America."

"Little did the poor woman know she would end up burying her husband next to her son, while she was here," lamented James.

"What has all of this got to do with me, Da? It's not the same now as it was in the old days. The Crown is slowly losing its grip on the country and there's a lot more support for the cause than ever there was before."

"I am very fond of Annie, son. She becomes more like one of my own daughters with each passing week, but I have always been wary of her family's involvement with the Fenians and of the influence they must surely have on you. Her brothers play hurling with you, so I take it they turn up for the *training* as well?"

"Of course they do, sure it was them put my name forward as captain of the team, and a fine pair of hurlers they are, too. But there are some things even more important than iománaíocht. Can you not see that we need to be trained and ready to do battle when the time is right, Da?"

James remained deep in thought for a few seconds before answering. "It's well known there are groups in every village in Ireland similar to yourselves and of the same mind. But there is another form of rebel that puts the fear of God in me, Jamie. The ones responsible for those dynamite explosions in England and Scotland, putting women and children at risk of losing life or limb. That is not an honourable way to conduct a war?"

"Are you speaking of those *infernal machines*? That has nothing to do with us, Da. Sure, most of the American Fenians themselves are against such acts."

"All I'm asking is that you be careful, son. Don't go letting others put you in positions they wouldn't take on themselves. You have a fire in you at times that reminds me of my old friend, Michael."

"Well, I shall take that as a compliment, Da."

James looked guardedly at the horizon.

"No, son. Take it as a warning."

CHAPTER SIXTEEN

The mattress may have been lumpy and the blankets rough but the bed Thomas woke up in had given him the best sleep in months. Judging by the snores coming from across the room, Petey was still enjoying his slumber. The heavy drapes had been left open to enable the first rays of sunlight to enter the room and rouse them before the town was awake and busy with people. Thomas was surprised to see Patrick sitting in a chair, staring through the window.

"How long have you been awake?" Thomas yawned and stretched.

"I never went to sleep. I'm surprised that cockerel didn't stir either of you, he was louder than Paddy Mac trying to clear his premises at the end of a busy night."

Patrick's words stabbed at Thomas with a sudden pang of homesickness and he allowed his thoughts to linger in the fishing village of his family, their faces as clear as if they stood before him.

"I think it best we wake up Petey now, if we are to catch the first stage out of here," said Patrick.

Thomas pulled himself upright, leaning his back against the timber wall at the head of his bed. "Leave him be for a few more minutes, Patrick, he has been through a tough year and could do with the extra bit of sleep."

Thomas went on to recount a story that had the hair standing up on Patrick's neck and set his blood boiling. Petey had been subjected to numerous beatings since his arrival at the mine. Patrick looked across at their sleeping companion and wondered how a man as slight as Petey could have survived such beatings, inflicted on him by Hannigan in his many drunken rages.

"Why did ye not get away sooner?" asked Patrick.

Thomas nodded in Petey's direction, "He wouldn't leave Dinny."

"What made Hannigan choose Petey? Was it because he was a coward and afraid to take on a bigger man?"

"Nothing of the sort, Patrick. Hannigan's cook is the mother of a young woman called Nell. He had taken her in from one of the saloons. I suppose he was the lesser evil and the two women felt in some way indebted to the man. Anyways, Nell took a shine to our Petey, sneaking him extra food and smiling at him at every opportunity. Hannigan found out about it and gave her a thrashing in front of Petey, to provoke him, and it worked. Well, you can guess who came out the worst?"

"Aye, poor old Petey."

"After that it became a macabre game that Hannigan liked to play to amuse himself," continued Thomas. "He treated them as if they were worthless, as he did everyone who worked for him. The story is that Hannigan himself was employed by the man that owns the coalmine and one day he found some gold. The coal itself paid well enough but gold was a different matter. Next thing anyone knows, Hannigan is in charge and the miners are leaving."

"I cannot blame them for doing so, Thomas."

"Those who remained did so because they owed money to the mine and their debts now belonged to Hannigan. He treated them no better than slaves, everyone except his henchmen, that is. I think, myself, that Hannigan was the victim of a confidence trick, for the cook told me he never did find any more gold in that mine.

"How did he die? Was it from the fever that you spoke of last night, the one his miners had come down with?" asked Patrick.

Thomas shook his head, "Hannigan did succumb to the same fever that had half his miners locked up in that shed to die. That was when I saw a chance to escape. I wrote that letter to William McIntyre and the cook sent it through the mail for me. But Hannigan's men were in fear of catching the fever themselves and had Dinny and Petey carry Hannigan to the shed. Then the two of them were locked in and told to look after him," Thomas glanced at their sleeping companion, "Dinny took care of him no doubt about that. During the night he held a pillow over his face while he slept. Bad and all as Hannigan was, Petey tried to stop Dinny from smothering him."

"Poor lad, we have to do our best to get him back to his family, Thomas. Do you think Hannigan's men are searching for ye? They must surely be aware of your absence by now."

"I haven't told you the worse part yet, Patrick. Nell came to me the night of Hannigan's funeral, while his henchmen drank themselves into a stupor, and told me something her mother had overheard earlier that day. She had returned to the kitchen to fetch a shawl, unbeknownst to the men, and heard them argue over the division of Hannigan's assets. We had assumed that with his death we would all be free to go but they had other plans."

Petey stirred and both men held their breath but his eyes remained closed as his breathing returned to the rhythm of a deep sleep.

"Go on, Thomas," Patrick poured some water from a jug into two tumblers and both men gulped the liquid down as if it were a shot of whiskey.

"Petey owes his life to those two women. I only wish we could have taken them with us. I did offer but Nell assured me they would be leaving soon enough themselves."

"What was it the girl's mother overheard, Thomas?"

"The men were intent on setting fire to the fever shed with everyone in it. Something even Hannigan, bad and all as he was, would never have done. They reasoned that it wouldn't be long before they themselves succumbed to the disease and it was the only way to ensure their own safety. Then they could get on with working the mine and making what profit was left in it, before the lease ran out. I daresay, they are still hopeful of finding gold."

Patrick was speechless as he let Thomas's words sink in. Neither man spoke until the silence was broken by the sound of movement from the rest of the house, a sign they wouldn't have too long to wait for their breakfast.

"As soon as I felt sure everyone was asleep or in a drunken slumber, I used the key that Nell had given me to let myself out of the quarters I had been kept in since my arrival at the mine. It was a terrible feeling locking that door again without alerting the rest of the men to their chance of escape, but it would have been too difficult for so many of us to get away unseen"

Patrick poured Thomas more water when he saw him bury his face in his hands, but left the glass by the jug on the nightstand when he heard the sound of muffled sobbing. Conscious of the time passing and even more aware of the importance of catching that first coach out of town, he reminded his brother-in-law of their present situation.

"I know, Patrick, I know. We've come this far and it's not the time to give in to feelings of self-pity and guilt. You see, I had not planned on telling Dinny or Petey what was in store for those sick men but Dinny was refusing to leave because they needed someone to look after them. Most of them couldn't even raise their heads to take a sip of water. Then Petey said he wouldn't go without him and all the while I was in fear of being discovered while they stood there arguing, so I drew out and punched young Petey so hard I knocked him out."

There was a sharp gasp from Patrick, who couldn't imagine Thomas being capable of such a thing, not even at the worst provocation.

"It was me gave Petey that black eye. Does that surprise you, Patrick? Imagine the shock I gave myself. I was so angry at him after all the trouble and danger I had gone through in finding him and there he was, arguing and wasting time. On an impulse I told Dinny what was about to befall the fever shed and that they were all going to die. There was no way we could carry the sick men to safety and now we had Petey lying on the floor between us."

The two men looked across at Petey, who was still fast asleep.

"Dinny might not have been the fastest on his feet but he was quick witted enough to realise the only way he could make sure that his young friend had any chance of escape was to help me carry him away from that place," Thomas continued. "We hadn't gone too far when Petey opened his eyes. We just kept running through the night after that and we were doing well until Dinny fell and broke his foot. The rest you already know, Patrick."

A loud rap on the door and a call for breakfast had Petey awake and on his feet in two seconds. The young man rubbed his eyes and looked from Patrick to Thomas as if trying to make out who they were.

"Oh bless us and save us! That knock made me think I was back at the mine."

CHAPTER SEVENTEEN

As the rain got heavier it became more difficult to make out what was being shouted across the field above the howl of the wind. Jamie slung his hurley over his shoulder and walked across the sodden grass to the man barking orders at them.

"McGrother, get back in line."

"Ahh, come on now, Sergeant Broderick. Sure, look at the state of us, soaked to the skin. I'm off to Paddy Mac's to dry out before I catch my death and if you've any sense, you'll order the men to do the same."

Jamie was relieved to see he was not the only one abandoning the training session, as men scarpered in all directions at the sight of him standing up to the sergeant. Two of them caught up with the young fisherman, matching his stride.

"He's still standing in the middle of the field, lads," Jamie had looked behind, "I'm not jesting, see for yourselves."

"We'll have hell to pay for this on the next session. That's your fault McGrother, he'll make us crawl on our bellies through the muckiest field he can find," complained one of the young men.

"I wish we could have a proper game, instead of all this marching and training we've been doing lately," the man on the other side of Jamie added to the grumbling.

"Listen now, lads. Training is what we signed up for and when we are called to action, we'll be glad of it. But I cannot see any sense in catching our deaths when there's no need. The sergeant won't push us that hard, for fear of losing us. He knows how fortunate he is to have us here at all, when half the men from the parish are across the water or in America. No doubt he'll be joining us later in Paddy Mac's."

By the time the trio had arrived at their destination the place was full of drenched bodies, competing for a spot by the open fire. Paddy Mac smiled at Jamie and held up a drink for him.

"My two friends here will have the same, Paddy, on me. They're a bit low in funds."

The men thanked Jamie and went back to join the crowd huddled around the roaring flames.

"I see the rain put a stop to the training, Jamie. Young fellas are very soft nowadays. In my time we carried on regardless of the weather," teased Paddy.

"It's alright to be running around training for a game, the excitement of it keeps your mind from the weather, Paddy. But this standing in line or hiding behind a hedge waiting on orders is senseless on a day such as this. We'll all end up sick and then there'd be no money to feed our families. Is the sergeant going to arrive on our doorsteps with a bowl of broth and a round of bread? I don't think so."

No sooner were the words out of Jamie's mouth, when the door opened and a hush fell over the place. Sergeant Broderick walked through the crowd to stand dripping beside the young fisherman at the bar.

"I take it we're finishing up the training here, then. Well, Paddy, if you'll be so kind as to serve up a steaming hot whiskey to a drowned rat, I would be much obliged."

Jamie patted the sergeant's back to the roar of men's laughter.

99

"Do you have a snug, Paddy? I'd like to have a quiet word with this young fella," Sergeant Broderick had lowered his voice.

The barman pointed to a door that opened into a small room, where women could drink apart from the men. Due to the inclement weather on that Sunday afternoon, it was empty and as James followed the sergeant into its cosy interior he shrugged his shoulders at Paddy Mac's questioning look.

"I hope I haven't offended you, Sergeant. I meant no disrespect leaving the field as I did and I was as surprised as yourself when the rest of the men did likewise."

For a moment, the sergeant looked at Jamie as if unsure of what he had just heard. His reply was a shock to the young man and a severe reprimand would have been more welcome.

"Offended me? Not at all, Jamie lad. Although, training in bad weather is something you will all have to get used to, we're not living in Spain, man," both men took a long drink from their glasses. "Would you be related in some way to my landlady, Miss McGrother?"

Jamie almost sprayed the other man with a mouthful of beer. "That depends on your motive for asking such a question," he replied.

"Now it's my turn to assure *you* that I mean no disrespect. I have already asked her the same question but she told me that it was none of my business. I get the feeling that you two are not overly fond of each other."

Jamie took another drink before responding. It wasn't like him to analyse his thoughts too much before answering a question but something told him, in this instance, he would be wise to do so.

"My sister and myself do not always see eye to eye on matters. Sure, isn't that the way it is with most families?" Jamie glanced up at a clock sitting on a shelf over the only window in the snug, "Speaking of women, my wife will be expecting me home any minute."

The sergeant was delighted to hear of the family connection between his landlady and Jamie. The response from the young man seemed to imply the siblings were at least on speaking terms.

"I wonder if you could do me a favour, Jamie. Would you put in a good word for me with your sister, the next time you see her? My intentions are honourable, I can assure you. I have only been here a fortnight but she has made a favourable impression on me."

Jamie was almost visibly squirming at the words he heard. To have to obey orders from a man who was smitten with one of his sisters was bad enough, but for it to be Mary-Anne was unthinkable. Before he could stop himself, words he should never have spoken spilled out of his mouth.

"I'm not so sure it would do you much good, Sergeant Broderick. My sister is not the woman you might think she is. Did you know she has a son, yet she has never been wed?" It was a scurrilous comment and Jamie knew it.

A galled look came over the older man's face and Jamie could not tell whether it was directed at himself or his sister.

"I would have expected more from you, young man, than to join in the vicious slander of such a fine woman – and your own flesh and blood at that. She has already confided in me as to how

101

young George came to be under her guardianship. It's a pity there are not more like her, willing to perform such charitable deeds," Sergeant Broderick stood up and drained his glass in a long swallow. "Go home to your wife, Jamie. I sincerely hope you treat her with more respect than you do your sister."

Left alone in the snug, Jamie seethed at the change in atmosphere created by the mere mention of his sister's name. Mary-Anne didn't even have to be in his company to ruin his day or make his stomach churn. The prospect of spending the rest of his days living in the same county, never mind the same village, as Mary-Anne, was a thorn in Jamie's side. He resolved there and then, if he could not bring himself to accept it, he would have to do something about it.

CHAPTER EIGHTEEN

The plan was to get to New York by rail but the most difficult part would be getting to the station in Pittsburg for the first part of their journey. In spite of the danger that might lie ahead for them, Petey had no trouble wolfing down a breakfast of ham and eggs. A plate sat in the middle of the table, piled high with biscuits and the young man glanced quickly at the other diners before swiping a handful to fill his pockets.

Thomas was just as hungry as Petey but refrained from an outward display of it, not wanting to draw any attention to their table. When he saw the younger man grab the biscuits he kicked his foot under the table and glared at him.

Patrick was picking at his breakfast, his appetite overwhelmed by their precarious situation. He would have liked Thomas to pay more attention to the door leading into the room, but knew how distracting a good meal could be to someone kept in a constant state of hunger for over a month. Being the only one among the trio who would not recognize any of Hannigan's men added to his anxiety.

"Could you please keep a better watch on the door, Thomas," Patrick leaned in close to whisper.

"It will be too late if they come through the door, Patrick," came the reply through a mouthful of ham, "We have no weapons and they will be well armed. I have my eye on the window to the street. Better to see the danger before it sees us."

Patrick leaned back in his chair and breathed a sigh of relief. Reassured that he was not the only one on high alert, he took another mouthful of breakfast and had hardly swallowed it when Thomas abruptly rose from the table, his eyes trained on the window.

"I think we need to finish packing our belongings," Thomas knew that Patrick would get the message.

"What belongings?" asked Petey.

Patrick stretched his leg out and dug his boot into the young man's shin, thankful to the landlady for an overly long tablecloth that looked so out of place in the bare wooden room. Petey was on his feet before Patrick and they followed Thomas through the door. As soon as they were back in their room the reason for such a hasty exit became clear.

"I saw Nell walk past the window and there was a man alongside her, with a tight grip on her arm," revealed Thomas.

"The woman who helped you escape? Was she with one of Hannigan's men?"

Thomas took a deep breath to calm his nerves, "Yes, Patrick. It was Nell but I can't say for sure who the man was, his hat was pulled down low over his face and he walked on the other side of her, away from the window."

Petey swallowed the food that had remained in his mouth since his shin had been kicked and looked on as Thomas paced the floor. He refused to believe they could get this far only to be captured again.

"Did you not say that Nell and her mother had planned on leaving, Thomas?" Petey's face lit up with a smile, "Sure that must be why she's in town. Maybe they're waiting on the stage, too, like us."

"I wish I could believe that, Petey, but I saw the stiffness in her walk and her arm was not being held in a friendly way by any means."

Grabbing the one bag they had between them, Patrick threw each man his hat and placed his own firmly on his head.

"We'd best be getting out of here, so. I'll settle the account with the landlady while you two make your way around to the street from the back."

Thomas opened the window, "Come on, Petey, you first."

Once they were alone in the room the two brothers-in-law embraced and Thomas extracted a promise from Patrick, that should he be captured, he was to go straight back to New York and this time inform the police about his circumstances, which had changed with the death of Hannigan.

"I'm truly sorry for getting you involved in this mess, Patrick. One of us must get back to our families, we cannot leave our children fatherless. I know you'll do right by Lily and the baby. Tell her I love her with all my heart and that I never stopped thinking of her, not even for a second. Will you do that for me, please?"

Patrick tried to reassure Thomas they would all be re-united with their loved ones again but before the words could leave his mouth, he found himself standing alone in the room, watching the curtains billow in the breeze from the open window.

The landlady handed a package wrapped in brown paper to Patrick when he paid the bill, telling him it was *a bite to eat on the journey*. In the street, he scanned the faces of every couple

105

he could see but knew it would be impossible for him to even guess which one of the women could be Nell. He noticed how most men held onto the arm of their female companions as they passed by groups of dusty, rough looking characters. The thought struck him that he was inclined to do so himself whenever he took a walk with his own wife.

One couple in particular held his attention, the girl evidently in an anxious state. As he drew closer, Patrick could see how tight a grip her companion had on her upper arm. Only once had he ever taken hold of Catherine in such a way and it was in a moment of anger. Patrick was sure the young woman was Nell and followed them to the next saloon.

Waiting outside, he watched for the couple to reappear and tried to make small talk with an old lady sitting in the shade of the eaves. She rocked back and forth in her chair, smoking a pipe, ignoring him, so Patrick assumed she was hard of hearing. As he bent low to shout into her ear, the man he had been following came back through the door, pulling a very distressed woman after him.

"Been watching him drag that young-un all over town for two days now. Seems in a mighty sour mood if you ask me," the old woman leaned forward and spat a brown glob of phlegm onto the dusty street below. "Reckon that poor girl is in fer the hiding of her life when he gits her home," she looked up at Patrick and spat again, this time aiming between his feet. "Men," she spewed out the word, "I've seen him with just about every saloon girl in town but when a woman gives him a taste of his own medicine he can't swaller it."

"Do they live in town, Ma'am?" Patrick thought he might be following the wrong couple.

The woman leaned forward, "He's one of them that's taken over Hartigan's coalmine. Stepped into a dead man's shoes – and his bed, by the looks of it. I reckon the man he's looking fer is long gone, if he has an ounce of sense."

"I sure wouldn't stay around too long, if I was him. It's been a pleasure talking Ma'am. Good day to you, now," Patrick raised his hat as he turned to retrace his steps back up the street to join his friends.

It was a fast walk that brought him to where he had arranged to meet Thomas and Petey. Although it had been very tempting to break into a run, the sight of a man racing through town might have attracted too much attention. Standing at the rear of the Dublin woman's lodging house, Patrick heard the sound of a familiar birdcall rise above the clucking of hens and smiled. When he entered the hen house he was relieved to find his two friends. They were hoping it was good news he carried with him but what they heard was both good and bad.

"It seems he's only looking for one of ye. He must think Petey died in the fire," said Patrick.

"What fire?" asked Petey.

The two older men looked at each other and Patrick wished he could take back his words. It was the wrong time to reveal the fate of those unfortunate men in the fever shed. All three of them needed to keep their wits about them and feelings of guilt and remorse would do nothing but cloud their judgement.

"I heard talk in the town of a fire at the mine," said Patrick.

"If I'm not being missed then it must have been the fever shed caught fire. Do you think one of the men inside knocked over a lantern, Thomas?"

"That's more than likely what happened, Petey. Maybe not all of them got out in time and it was taken that you and Dinny were among the victims of the fire. Sure isn't that good news for you. Nobody will be on your trail now," assured Thomas.

"The same cannot be said about you, Thomas," said Patrick, "You must have been missed the next morning. The old woman says that man has been scouring the town for the past two days, looking for someone he claims had his way with the girl."

Petey looked aghast at Thomas, momentarily forgetting his grief over the tragic events at the mine.

"For heaven's sake, Petey. Do you think I would do a thing like that to young Nell? Someone must have seen her collect the keys from where I left them," said Thomas. "I'll wager there's more than one of those henchmen in town. They'll be watching the stage, for sure. What do we do now?"

"First of all, we must find Petey a good hiding place," replied Patrick. "Should anything happen to us, there will be no reason for them to continue watching the stage. You must do your best to be on it when it sets off, Petey, even if we are not with you."

In spite of his protest that he would not leave town without his companions, Petey agreed to hide in the crawl space underneath the small wooden church, where they had met up the previous evening, and await their return.

"You have the parcel of food with you for tonight but save some for your breakfast, Petey. Keep a lookout for tomorrow's stage and if we are nowhere to be seen, you must board it yourself. Remember to pull your hat down low over your brow and if you think the coach is being watched, go back into hiding and try again next day. Give me your word on that now, before we part." Patrick placed some money in the young man's hand, "This is enough to get you to Pittsburgh and the price of a train journey to New York."

"I cannot do such a thing. I am not leaving without either of you."

"You can and you will, lad," Thomas went on to give Petey the address of the newspaper he was employed by. "Tell them you have a message from Thomas McGrother and ask to see Mr. McIntyre. He'll know what to do."

As Petey was about to protest once more, Patrick grabbed the front of the young man's shirt and yanked him towards him.

"I'll be damned if one of us doesn't get back to New York, so you had best make sure you are on that stage tomorrow, Petey. If anything should happen to Thomas or myself, do you think we would want our efforts to get you home to have been in vain?"

All Petey could do was shake his head and Patrick was surprised to see tears fill his eyes. He embraced his young friend, holding him tight for a few seconds. "Good man, it's for the best this way," he said, releasing him.

Thomas stepped forward and did likewise, "Sure we've made it this far, Petey, even if we're not on that stage in the morning, there's no reason to think we cannot find our way to Pittsburgh by other means."

CHAPTER NINETEEN

Maggie watched her niece's approach, admiring the confident walk and self-assured demeanour of the young woman, who was well aware of the whispers behind her back. Mary-Anne had a ready smile and friendly salute for all who looked in her direction. It was amusing to see the village gossips being completely disarmed by her charm.

"Sit yourself down here, girl," Maggie patted the space on the wall between herself and Mary.

Mary-Anne kissed her mother's cheek and ran a caustic eye over her aunt, "And what has you smiling like the cat that got the cream this afternoon, Aunt Maggie?"

"That's no way to be speaking to your elders, Mary-Anne," Mary interceded before a row could take hold, "Isn't it a grand day altogether? Are you taking a rest from your work, love?"

"I saw you both here on the wall and decided to join ye. The bit of fresh air will do me good, I've been working my fingers to the bone all morning," Mary-Anne held out her hands to examine them.

"I hear you've been working someone else's fingers to the bone – along with your own, of course," said Maggie.

"Has Annie been complaining of her workload to you? I'm surprised she's even told you."

The two older women gasped and Mary-Anne knew by their expressions that her words had been a shock. She silently berated herself for carelessly revealing the secret arrangement she had made with her younger brother's wife. Annie was a diligent worker, whose company Mary-Anne found increasingly pleasant. She hoped her momentary lapse of discretion would not result in the loss of her help or her friendship.

It was unusual for Maggie to be lost for words, but it was Mary who spoke next, "She was speaking of young George. He was complaining of having to help you change the bedding. Your Da made us laugh, telling him it was no job for a man and he should be fetching the pail of water from the pump with the fine muscles he has on his little arms."

"So it's my father I have to blame for my son's bit of drama this morning," Mary-Anne laughed. "George snatched the pail from my hand and made off to the pump before he'd even taken his breakfast. Poor wee lad, I stood watching him from the window for a good five minutes as he struggled to carry it back. He was inching it forward at such a slow pace, it would have been this evening before I had any water for Ann . . ." Mary-Anne stopped abruptly.

An awkward silence followed and before Maggie had the chance to ask any questions, Mary stood and brushed some grains of sand from her black skirt.

"Speaking of water, I've a terrible thirst on me for a sup of tea. Come along, Maggie, it takes you as long to walk home on those bad legs of yours as it does young George to fetch a pail of water for his mother," Mary handed her sister-in-law the two walking sticks that helped to keep her mobile.

The humour had broken the tension and Mary-Anne stood still for a moment, her eyes following the two women as they slowly made their way towards the edge of the village. It would only be a matter of time before one of them, most likely Maggie, would let the cat out of the bag about

Annie's secret visits to her sister-in-law's lodging house. It was time for Mary-Anne to put her foot down and demand her brother be informed of their arrangement.

"Annie, Annie," she called upon entering the house.

The young woman came running through the kitchen doorway, "What is it, Ma'am?" she remembered the title she must use during her working hours.

Mary-Anne led Annie back into a kitchen filled with the pleasant aroma of freshly baked biscuits. It was another reminder as to why she must keep Annie in her employment at all cost.

"I take it you still have not informed your husband of our arrangement, have you?"

Shaking her head as she busied herself taking another tray from the oven, Annie promised that she would do so that coming weekend.

"That will be too late, my dear. You must tell him as soon as you get home. In fact, you should go right now, this very minute," Mary-Anne began to untie the large bow at the back of Annie's apron.

"Why must I be in such haste, Jamie is more than likely still asleep. I would much rather wait until Sunday, Mary-Anne – sorry – Ma'am. Oh you have me all flustered now."

Mary-Anne apologized for being so abrupt and explained how she had let it slip about Annie's work. "So you see, it won't be long until he finds out and it would be much better if it came from you than one of your neighbours or, worse still, one of his friends. I don't know how we've managed to keep it a secret for this long, even George doesn't know about it."

"It had to happen sooner or later, sure the biggest gossip in Blackrock lives just two doors away from you. The reason she hasn't found out about my working here is because I always use the back entrance and she's too busy sitting in her chair at the front, taking in what's going on in the street," Annie gave a deep sigh as she pulled the apron over her head.

"I'll pay you in full for today, Annie, and don't argue about it. I feel responsible for your distress and I hope you'll manage to talk that bull-headed brother of mine around."

Annie took her sister-in-law by surprise when she hugged her tight and kissed her cheek. "I'm very grateful for the work, Mary-Anne, and you're not to be feeling so guilty about giving it to me. Jamie will rant and rave and might very well break some of my crockery while doing so. But I will stand my ground and when his temper has cooled a bit, he will see how well my stubbornness matches his own."

Taking a cracked china cup and matching plate from the kitchen dresser, Mary-Anne handed them to Annie. "Put your crockery in a safe place and leave these old cracked ones to hand. Give him a good breakfast before you tell him. Men take bad news much better on a full stomach."

No amount of food could have lessened the impact of Annie's words on her husband's humour that morning. The sight of a plate full of poached eggs and freshly baked bread did wonders to lift his spirit but it was a much larger breakfast than usual and Jamie was puzzled by such extravagance.

"That was a feast fit for a king, love. I could barely finish it. Is there a reason why you've given me every egg the hens laid this morning?" he leaned back in his chair, massaging a full stomach.

Annie was worried she had gone overboard on the breakfast, causing her husband to expect bad news, but when she sat across from him at the table she was relieved to see a smile of satisfaction on his face. He looked so handsome when he was happy, for a moment her heart melted and she almost changed her mind about revealing her secret.

Jamie, on the other hand, had come to the conclusion that he was about to hear news of a baby and was relishing the thought of telling his father.

"I've been keeping something from you, Jamie. I tried to tell you before now but there never seemed to be a good time."

The young husband reached across the table and took hold of his wife's hands. "I know what you are about to tell me and I couldn't be more pleased for you, my love. Are you not as happy about it, yourself?"

The relief flooding through her took a heavy weight from her shoulders and Annie kissed the rough hands that held her own. "Oh, Jamie, you're the best husband in Ireland. How did you come to know my secret? Did someone tell you, or did you follow me one morning when I thought you were in bed?"

Jamie assumed his wife was speaking of morning sickness and must have been leaving the house to avoid alerting him to her condition. It made him love her all the more and he squeezed her hands reassuringly.

Not waiting for an answer, Annie continued, "Mary-Anne will be so pleased. Will you come with me to give her the good news? Can we go now, this minute?"

A sudden chill took hold of Jamie, as if a bucket of ice cold water had been thrown over his head. He was shocked at the warmth in his wife's voice as she spoke about his sister, and unconsciously tightened his grip on the small hands encased in his own.

By the dark look sweeping over his face Annie knew one of them had misunderstood the other. She winced as her hands were crushed and tried to shake them free. Jamie tightened his hold even more and pulled her arms across the table.

"What has you so eager to drag me to someone whose name I cannot even bear to hear, let alone share our happy news with?" Jamie released his wife's hands and stood up from the table. "She will hear about it soon enough. We shall call to my parents' house, they should be the first to know. Or have you told Ma, already?" Jamie managed a weak smile.

Rubbing her aching hands together, Annie replayed their conversation again in her head. There was something very wrong with Jamie's response and the reason why hit her like a bolt of lightning. "Do you think I'm with child? Is that why you sat beaming across the table at me, before I spoke of Mar.... I mean, of your sister?"

"Is that not what you've been trying to tell me? What other good news could it be? Have we come into a small fortune? Or perhaps the Queen herself is coming to tea, should I get into my good shirt?" Jamie leaned forward, his hands flat on the table.

The sarcasm was not lost on Annie and she kept her head bent as she responded in a quiet voice, purposely mentioning Mary-Anne's name. The words hit Jamie like a rock and he reeled back so quickly it looked as if he might fall over his chair.

Steadying both his balance and his nerve, Jamie asked Annie to repeat her words, he could not believe she was capable of such deceit. Waiting for her to speak, he curled his fingers around the bone china cup he had been drinking from. The fine breakfast his wife had surprised him with earlier, now sat like a lump of lead in Jamie's gut.

"I have been working at your sister's lodging house."

"BEHIND MY BACK?" roared Jamie.

Annie never even flinched. Rising from her chair and pulling herself up to her full height, she looked straight into his eyes, determined to stand her ground.

"Never raise your voice to me like that again, Jamie McGrother."

Annie noticed how white Jamie's knuckles had become with the grip he had on his cup. She prepared herself for the crash of its landing wherever he was about to throw it and struggled to keep from smiling at Mary-Anne's prediction. Curious as to how much more rage her husband was capable of, Annie was tempted to tell him whose cup it was he had such a tight hold of. She and her sister had grown up in a family of boys and learned from an early age not to fear their brothers' quick tempers and loud protests.

117

Jamie's arm began to tremble as he directed his anger and frustration into the hand grasping the cup. With a loud crack it shattered and large drops of blood began to fall on top of the broken crockery. Pulling a cloth from a line that hung over the fireplace, Annie placed it on the table between them.

"You'd best wash out that cut and make sure none of your sister's china is left in it – that cup was a present from Mary-Anne."

Jamie watched speechlessly as Annie took her shawl from the back of the door and wrapped it tightly around her shoulders.

"You'll find me at my parents' house when you have calmed down enough to speak to me with a bit of respect, Jamie."

The young husband looked away as the door closed behind his wife and turned his attention to the neatly folded cloth she had set before him. Next to it, lay the plate she had served up his breakfast on and he noticed how its pattern matched the one on the broken cup. A fresh wave of anger ran through him as Mary-Anne's taunting smile came into his head.

Annie heard the sound of the plate shattering as she walked by the open window.

CHAPTER TWENTY

"That's one of them, right enough. I reckon there's at least one more. The other two will be guarding the men back at the mine," Thomas whispered to Patrick as they drew away from the saloon window and crossed to the opposite side of the street. "He'll not be too much trouble, he can hardly sit upright with the drink, never mind stand. I don't see Nell anywhere inside, she must be with the other one."

"We could steal a couple of horses and send them back once we're near enough to the next town," suggested Patrick.

"And get ourselves shot in the process? No, we'll be on that stage tomorrow morning with Petey. In the meantime, we have to get your man over yonder drunk enough to pass out. Do you think you can do that, Patrick?"

"That won't take too long, he's halfway there already, but what are you planning on doing with the other one?"

"Let's deal with this one first and worry about that later. Will our funds stretch to plying him with plenty of strong liquor?" asked Thomas.

Patrick nodded, "We can do without a meal or two. It will be worth the sacrifice."

Having agreed to meet back where Petey was hiding, the two men shook hands, wishing each other luck. Thomas hoped that Patrick would not try to deal with the other man alone, he knew those men would not hesitate to kill him, should he cause them any trouble.

Petey was more than happy to have Thomas's company and offered him some food from the parcel the landlady had given them, "I never even took a bite out of it. I've been hoping to share it with the both of ye."

"Let's save it for when Patrick is with us, shall we Petey?" Thomas replied, hoping their wait would not be in vain.

It wasn't long before a low whistle announced their friend's arrival and Petey found himself once again alone in his hiding place. Thomas followed Patrick to an unoccupied bench outside a securely locked general store, wooden shutters drawn across its windows. It was a good vantage point from which to view the entire length of the main street.

"The merchant that owns this place told me he closes his store early on the days the miners get paid. I can see why, the town is already full of men so drunk they wouldn't recognize their own mother. There's no need to worry about your man either, he'll not be causing us any trouble, Thomas."

"Tell me you didn't do him any harm, Patrick. Those men are all brothers and thick as thieves – you injure one and the four of them feel it."

"I know, Thomas, you don't have to keep reminding me. I do not relish the thought of them following me back to my family, if we manage to escape from this hellish place. What of the men they hold captive back at the mine, their plight has been playing on my conscience?"

"Once I am back in New York I shall do everything in my power to have that place shut down. I know whose ear to put the right words into and it will be to their advantage, politically speaking, to investigate the goings on at that mine," Thomas pulled his hat even lower as he spoke.

Leaning forward, Patrick rested his elbows on his knees and clasped his hands tightly together, his eyes never leaving the street, "By all accounts, according to my *friend* who now rests in a drunken slumber, those four will be long gone by the time you bring their deeds to light. The lease is soon to run out on that old mine and the family of the original owner are itching to get their hands on it again."

"That must have been why Hannigan kept Petey and those other unfortunate men as no more than slaves. Got up to his old tricks, he did, when time began to run out on him. By keeping them indebted to him, he had the legal right to extract payment in kind by way of their labour, especially as they had put their mark on a contract," Thomas paused to make sure nobody was within hearing distance, "That was how I came to be among those poor unfortunates. The sheriff is the one who pointed me in the direction of Hannigan's mine when I enquired about work, and Nell told me he is a regular visitor to the place – collecting his share of the profit, no doubt."

"Was that why you warned against getting the police involved, in your letter to Mr. McIntyre?"

"It was, Patrick."

A couple crossing the street, some distance away, caught both men's eyes.

"That's himself and Nell, is it not?" asked Patrick.

Thomas nodded, "You are sure he will not come across his brother?"

"I talked him into accompanying me to another saloon and once he had passed out from the drink I paid the price of a bed for two nights and made sure he would be given plenty of time to sleep it off. He'll not be disturbed until we are well away from here."

"Well then, we shall have to handle this one in a similar manner. I'm afraid you will have to make his acquaintance, Patrick," Thomas pulled some leaves from a weed growing along the side of the wooden building and formed them into a wad, "Here, wrap some notes around this. It will fool him into thinking you've more money than sense. Likely he will want to take advantage of a gombeen Irishman, fresh off the boat, if you understand my meaning."

"I do indeed, Thomas, and I can act the eejit as well as any man when the need arises. Catherine will tell you that, herself," laughed Patrick. "Wait for me around the back, behind the stables. It may take a while, if he can hold his drink as well as his brother. I shall be out to relieve myself no doubt, so listen for my signal."

Once inside the crowded saloon, it didn't take Patrick too long to find his man. The scowl on his face was enough to ward off even the toughest of men. In the guise of someone fresh from the green fields of Ireland seeking his fortune, Patrick sat at the table of the rough looking man and the anxious young woman. He beamed the most idiotic smile he could muster at them.

"Well now, isn't this a grand place altogether," Patrick waved at one of the saloon girls, who carried a tray in her hand.

The angry scowl left the man's face as soon as he caught sight of the wad of money Patrick took from inside his waistcoat.

"Will you do me the honour of joining me in a drink, sir? And yourself, ma'am? Will you be having a wee drop of something or would you prefer a cup of tea?" asked Patrick.

If her situation hadn't been so grave, Nell would have laughed. Instead she tried to think of a way to warn off the naïve Irishman before he got himself into the kind of trouble that could see him lose more than just his wad of cash. Before Nell could say a word, her companion took hold of her wrist, squeezing it so tight the blood almost stopped.

"She's had enough, can't hold her drink. Can you, Nell? As for me," he looked around the saloon with an arrogant smirk, "I can drink any man here under the table and so could my brother, if I could find him."

As the night wore on, the talk flowed as freely as the alcohol and Patrick feared he may well run out of money before accomplishing his task. Staying sober was not too difficult, as he made sure to fill the other man's glass to the brim from the whiskey bottles placed between them on the table.

Nell had noticed the much smaller amounts of alcohol consumed by Patrick but made no mention of it. She assumed he was up to some sort of a con and resolved to keep on the alert to make good her escape, as soon as her captor was drunk enough to take his eye off her.

"Are you a good Irish Catholic, sir?" the rough-looking man leaned forward, swaying.

"I am, indeed. But it's not too easy to find a priest in these parts, that's for sure, and I'm badly in need of absolution for some terrible sins I would never have committed at home in my own parish," Patrick slurred his words as he made the sign of a cross over his heart. "My poor mother would turn in her grave at what I've been doing since I stepped off that boat."

An evil grin spread across the other man's face and he grabbed a handful of Nell's dark curls, yanking her head around to face Patrick.

"How's about adding a few more sins to your load, before you meet that priest and he forces you to mend your ways. Nell here can help you out – for a price."

Patrick didn't have to make any pretence at being shocked. The man's proposition came as a total surprise but Nell's expression told him it wasn't the first time she had been degraded in such a manner. With the hair pulled back from her face, Patrick noticed dark bruising around her left temple. He was about to protest when a thought occurred to him.

"I – ahem –," Patrick licked his dry lips as he furtively looked around, "I'm sure one more sin won't make too much of a difference at this stage – that is if the young lady doesn't mind."

"The *young lady* will do as she's told and don't take any nonsense from her. I'll pay the barman for an hour upstairs. By the eager look on your face you'll barely need five minutes."

Placing some money on the open palm in front of him, Patrick asked if it was enough.

"It will do. She's in a sour mood this evening so you'll not be getting the best out of her," the man gave the young woman such an evil look, it sent shivers through Patrick. "You behave yourself, Nell. The gentleman has paid good money for your time. Off you go then, woman, you know which room it is by now."

Things were not going according to plan and this was something Patrick had not anticipated.

There was no option but to follow her up the well-worn steps at the back of the saloon and once out of view from below, introduce himself, explaining what he was up to.

"He's going to wait until we are in bed and then surprise you with a blow to the back of your head. That was a foolish thing you did, taking out a wad of money in full view of everyone," Nell admonished.

"I meant for him to see it. I knew greed would get the better of him, although I didn't expect this." Patrick got flustered, "I mean, I'm grateful for the offer but I'm wed to a very good woman, as pretty as yourself, so . . .,"

Nell smiled and lightly stroked his cheek, stemming the flow of words. "I'm not offended," she whispered.

"I'd best be going, so," muttered Patrick. "Lock the door behind me and wait for my return, it should not be long before your friend is in the same drunken stupor as his brother and I shall get the barman to help me carry him up to you."

When Patrick reached the top of the stairs he saw that the table he had been seated at was occupied by four men, arguing over a card game. The barman was too pre-occupied with a thirsty crowd to notice anyone's comings and goings but Patrick had no intention of taking any chances.

'He must have gone outside to relieve himself,' Patrick reasoned, before climbing through an open window at the top of the stairs.

It was the sound of horses being disturbed that caught his attention the moment Patrick hit the ground, at the rear of the noisy saloon. A short sprint brought him to where the animals were stabled and he could tell that something was spooking them. The sound of a man grunting came from behind the shed and Patrick almost fell over at what he saw taking place there.

Thomas was struggling to pull a soaking wet man from a horse trough and Patrick instinctively went to his aid. When they pulled him free he took a fit of coughing as they lay him face down on the ground, and Patrick realized it was the man he had come to look for. "How did he fall in?" he asked, anxiously looking around.

"I came up behind him when he relieved himself and hit him over the head with that," Thomas pointed to a plank of wood lying on the ground a few yards away. "I don't know if it was the drink or the blow that made him sway so much, but he staggered and landed in the trough."

Patrick knew what had to be done and there would be no time to argue with his brother-in-law about it. "Go back to the stable and keep an eye out for anyone coming this way. We don't have much time."

Thomas was horrified to see Patrick remove the man's gun from its holster, "You can't shoot him, someone will hear. Besides, the sheriff will find out soon enough who it is that he's been looking for and then I'll really be in trouble."

"I'm not going to shoot him, Thomas. That bit of wood isn't thick enough to knock out a fly never mind a man his size. A sharp blow in the right place will have him out cold long enough for us to get away," Patrick spun the weapon in his hand, to grab hold of its long nozzle.

"Oh, I see. I suppose we had better tie him up and gag him so. Shall I fetch some rope from the stable?"

126

Patrick was sitting on the man's back at this stage, "You do that, Thomas," he said, raising the gun in the air.

One blow was all it took for the body beneath him to slump into unconsciousness. Patrick knew he would have to act quickly, before his brother-in-law's return, and dragged the helpless man to the deep trough.

Taking a good look around to make sure he wasn't being observed, Patrick lifted the heavy weight as if it were one of the large blocks of stone from the quarry where he worked.

"I'm sorry, man, but you've left me no choice. May God have mercy on your soul – and mine," he said in a quiet voice.

On his return, Thomas dropped the rope and began to run towards the body floating face down in the trough. He was yanked back and dragged into the stables by Patrick, setting the horses off again.

"Calm yourself down, man, you're making the horses uneasy. It had to be done, Thomas. This way it looks like an accident, he could have hit his head falling into the trough. The barman can vouch for how drunk he was and as far as he knows, I am still upstairs with Nell."

For a moment, Thomas was rendered speechless by what he had seen and heard. "You drowned him, Patrick. I cannot believe you would do such a thing to a man too drunk to defend himself. We could have tied him up and made good our escape. Have you murdered his brother, too? And why were you in a room with Nell?"

Losing patience, Patrick led Thomas to the spot under the window that he had jumped from earlier and told him to help him up. It was important that he be seen to come down the stairs with Nell, especially by the barman.

Lifting his foot onto the interlocked hands of his brother-in-law, Patrick promised that he would explain everything to him later and told him to get back to Petey and to make sure he was not followed.

Back in the room with Nell, Patrick confessed to what he had done and received a kiss for his trouble.

"Tell me where you have left his brother and I will make sure he stays drunk enough to forget why he came to town in the first place. By the time he sobers up, you will be long gone."

"But what will become of you, Nell? Come with us, New York is a big city and a person can easily lose themselves there."

Nell shook her head and gave Patrick a sad smile, "Your offer is very tempting but I must go back to my mother. She has already arranged a journey for us, to her brother in California. Now that Hartigan is gone, it shall not be long before the mine is abandoned," as she stepped into the corridor, Nell linked her arm through Patrick's. "Now, remember to wear that stupid grin on your face again as we go down the stairs. The barman will expect you to look like the cat that got the cream."

CHAPTER TWENTY-ONE

Mary-Anne silently berated herself as she dried the last piece of crockery and placed it on the kitchen dresser. It had been tempting to hire a replacement for Annie as soon as it became apparent that Jamie would make life difficult for both of them, but she could be just as stubborn as her younger brother.

A message had been delivered to Mary-Anne the evening before by one of Annie's brothers, informing her that the young woman had taken ill and would be unable to work the following morning but she hoped to be well on the mend in a day or two. Annie assured Mary-Anne that she would understand if someone else was hired to replace her but she hoped that would not be the case. When questioned about the state of her health, the young man had remarked that his sister looked more angry than ill when she arrived at his parents' house. He reckoned she must have had a row with her husband, "The first of many, no doubt, knowing our Annie." His parting words had played on Mary-Anne's mind for the rest of the evening, causing her sleep to be fitful and broken.

How quickly she had taken to her sister-in-law was just as much of a surprise to Mary-Anne as it had been to Annie. Both women felt a respect for each other that had not taken very long to form. On the surface, they appeared very different in character but there was a determination and boldness in their nature that each one recognized and admired in the other. The extra workload was a sacrifice Mary-Anne was willing to make, even if it lasted for the rest of the week, in order to keep Annie in her employ.

Sergeant Broderick noticed with concern how tired his landlady appeared to be that morning, as she served him breakfast. The eggs were boiled as hard as rocks, as if they had been left on the hot stove and forgotten about. He could see by the wisps of dark hair, escaping her normally neatly tied bun, that Mary-Anne must have been working extra hard in the kitchen. Deciding not to complain about the eggs, the sergeant broke the top off the first one. The result would have been neater had he used a fret saw, rather than a knife.

"Will you join me for breakfast, ma'am. It would make a pleasant start to my day. I have some eggs to spare."

Mary-Anne looked at the dense, solid yoke and apologized profusely for serving the apparent culinary disaster. She snatched up the plate, annoyed with herself for making such a simple mistake. Since his arrival, the sergeant had been complimenting her on the perfect consistency of his egg yolk, exactly the way he liked it, soft but not too runny.

"Have you been coping with an extra workload this morning, Ma'am?" Sergeant Broderick stood to take the plate from her hands, "I did not mean to complain about the food, I was merely assuring you that I had enough here for both of us. Please do not go to any more trouble, except to fetch an extra place setting for my table. I would be much obliged for the company."

The sergeant was standing in front of his landlady, both of them still holding onto the plate. The close proximity was as unnerving to Mary-

Anne as it was pleasant to him. He discreetly inhaled the faint smell of lavender that constantly hung about her presence and waited patiently as she calculated how much time she had to spare.

"Right so, I think I can take a few minutes to share that pot of tea with you. I'll go fetch a cup and saucer."

As she entered the kitchen, Mary-Anne caught a glimpse of herself in a mirror and realised what it was that made the sergeant aware of how busy her morning had been. Having removed her apron, she tidied away the loose strands of hair and put a friendly smile on her face, before returning to the dining room looking fresh as a daisy.

The sergeant held out a chair for her and she couldn't help but notice how pleased he was with her decision to join him. The attention he had been giving her since his arrival at her lodging house had not been lost on Mary-Anne but there was something else about him that was beginning to break through her tough veneer.

As Sergeant Broderick spoke about his army days Mary-Anne paid more heed to his physical features than his eventful life. She had the strongest urge to find out how old he was but knew it would sound much too forward to ask outright

"I do apologize for going on about such a boring subject, Ma'am. Please forgive me, I'm not accustomed to female company," the sergeant had become aware of Mary-Anne's abstraction.

"There's nothing to forgive, Sergeant Broderick, I find your story very interesting indeed. I was wondering how long you've been retired. It must be quite recent – you still have the army way about you. You make your own bed every morning," Mary-Anne lifted the cloth to look beneath the table. "And your boots are so well polished, I can see my reflection in them."

The sergeant let out a hearty laugh, "I ran away from home to become a soldier when I was barely thirteen," he leaned forward to whisper as if someone might be eavesdropping, "I lied about my age. I've been gone from the army now for more than ten years, my mother needed me to come home and take care of the family business. She was not in the best of health and my father was dying."

"I'm so sorry for your loss, I'm sure it was of great comfort to your poor mother to have you with her at such a sad time. It must have been distressing for you to leave a way of life you had become so accustomed to."

The sergeant sat back in his chair and stared in wonder at Mary-Anne. He had never come across a woman quite like her before, with such a tough outer shell yet capable of genuine empathy.

The strange look on his face unnerved Mary-Anne. "I must apologize to you again, Sergeant Broderick. I did not mean to cause offence, I have a bad habit of speaking before thinking."

"Oh no, Ma'am. I was not offended. Your words took me by surprise, you are the first person to acknowledge that I lost more than a parent when my father died. The army had been my life for twenty-five years. It was not an easy decision to make, by any means, but I was duty bound to do right by my mother."

Mary-Anne quickly calculated that the man whose company she was fast becoming very comfortable in, was at least eighteen years her senior.

"I take it you have no brothers or sisters, so?" she asked.

"I was their only surviving child, my younger brother and sister both died within a few months of each other from scarlet fever. I was at boarding school and was spared the same fate. My parents took me home after my brother died and began to stifle me with the same amount of affection that had previously been shared between three of us. I begged to be sent back to school but my father insisted that I learn the family business – he was a baker. It wasn't very long before I ran off to join the army."

Mary-Anne rose abruptly at the mention of baking, realising she had not prepared the lunch promised to two of her guests. Explaining that she had a great deal of work to do, the young woman excused herself and bade a hurried farewell to the sergeant.

Left alone at his table, Sergeant Broderick replayed the conversation again in his head, worrying that he had revealed too much about himself, too soon. It was not something he was in the habit of doing, being a very private person. Mary-Anne had somehow loosened a tongue that was usually tied in a knot when it came to conversing with pretty young women.

Meanwhile, in the kitchen a very perturbed Mary-Anne tried to shake the warm feeling her encounter with the sergeant had created. As she struggled to focus on the meal she was late in preparing, his voice remained in her head.

"I'm sorry to bother you, Ma'am, but I thought I might save you the trouble."

Mary-Anne swung around to see her lodger place his crockery on the kitchen table and was taken aback at how the years seemed to have dropped away from his face. The sergeant's thoughtful gesture may have been a display of good manners on his part but to Mary-Anne it had a much more sinister meaning. His next words almost sent her fleeing from the house.

"Could you use a bit of help? I'm a dab hand in the kitchen."

A quick glance from Mary-Anne towards the open back door caused Sergeant Broderick to retreat into the hallway. He could see how much his presence had disturbed her but misread the reason.

"Now it is my turn to apologize. I did not think how it might appear if I were to be discovered with you, alone in your kitchen. We must always be wary of the gossip mongers, is that not so, Ma'am?"

The sergeant gave a stiff bow before turning sharply on his heel, leaving Mary-Anne alone to deal with her racing heart and mixed emotions.

CHAPTER TWENTY-TWO

Thomas concentrated on the landscape rushing past the window of the railway carriage and tried to silence his disturbing thoughts. Quickly glancing at Patrick but not wanting to catch his eye, he saw that his brother-in-law was sleeping, head resting against the glass. Petey was seated next to him, wide awake, finishing off the remainder of a cake they had purchased at the station.

"Did you want some, Thomas? Only, Patrick said I could eat it," the words were mumbled through a mouthful of food.

"No thank you, Petey. I've had more than enough," Thomas turned towards the window.

"Is there something the both of ye are keeping from me?" Petey's voice was barely above a whisper.

The younger man had switched seats to sit beside Thomas and was looking in the same direction, at nothing in particular.

"Why would you think such a thing, Petey? Of course not."

"Ye have been acting mighty strange ever since we got on that stage. At first I put it down to nerves, due to the situation we were in and the fear we had of being set upon," Petey's eyes fell on Patrick, sleeping undisturbed opposite them. "But we are well away from danger now, you said so yourself, Thomas, and yet there is an uneasiness between the two of ye that was never there before."

Thomas was surprised by the younger man's intuition.

"We're exhausted, Petey. I'm sure I shall sleep for a week, once I am home," Thomas feigned a yawn. "I'm surprised you're not in a deep slumber, yourself," he leaned his head back and closed his eyes, hoping to end the conversation.

As the train rumbled on, Petey watched his two friends closely and came to the conclusion that what Thomas had said about them being weary was not the only reason for the chill he felt had come between them. They still treated him with the same warmth and friendliness as before.

If the brothers-in-law needed to speak to each other in private there had been no opportunity to do so up to that point, as the trio had been wary of separating, even for the shortest period of time.

Petey kicked Patrick's feet and he woke up with a jolt, a look of alarm on his face.

"What's happened? Are we almost there?" he scanned the countryside in the distance.

Leaning forward, Petey apologized for disturbing his sleep and whispered something in his ear that left Patrick staring coldly at Thomas. He shook his brother-in-law by the shoulder.

"Is it true, what Petey says?" he asked, but there was no response.

"Thomas, I know you can hear me," Patrick shook him again.

"What did Petey say that's so important?" Thomas's eyes remained closed as he spoke.

"I told Patrick you would be leaving us at the next stop."

Thomas opened his eyes to glare at Petey, "And why would you say such a thing, when it's not true?"

"Well, now that ye are both awake, I think it's time to deal with whatever it is that's bothering

136

ye. I shall be stretching my legs for a while. Or would it be wiser for ye to take a walk yourselves?" Petey replied.

The older men stared at him in surprise and it was a few seconds before one of them spoke.

"There is something I must discuss with you, Patrick, before we are reunited with our families," Thomas rose from his seat. "It would be best to speak of it in private, as Petey suggested."

Before following Thomas from the carriage, Patrick gave his young friend a warning, "I do not take kindly to my sleep being disturbed, Petey, and I may very well be even more irritated on my return than I am this minute."

By the time Patrick had joined Thomas outside their carriage he was ready to hear whatever it was that caused the rift in their friendship. Petey had not been the only one to have noticed it.

"Well? What do you have to say for yourself, Thomas?"

"I could ask you the same question, Patrick."

"This kind of talk will get us nowhere, I'm going back inside."

Thomas grabbed his brother-in-law by the arm as he made to turn away, "I'm sorry for my coolness towards you, Patrick. It was childish of me to behave in such a manner."

"Coolness? I've felt less of a chill without my coat on a winter's day in New York. Has this to do with that fella's drowning, by any chance?"

Thomas lost his composure, "You killed a man, Patrick. One that I was trying to save. Do you not feel any remorse?"

Although Patrick had a fair idea why there had been such a coolness between them, Thomas's words were hard to take.

"Do you think he would have been so grateful to you for sparing his life that he would have shaken your hand and let us all walk away in peace?" asked Patrick.

"He may have, but you didn't give him an opportunity to show it, did you? What disturbs me is how easily you made such a decision about another man's life and the fact that even now, you display no remorse."

A thought struck Patrick and before he could stop himself the words were out, "I see. So you think because I was the cause of a man's death in the past – accidentally, I hasten to add – that I am a cold hearted murderer?"

"That is not what I said," replied Thomas.

"Ahh, but it's what you've been thinking – and don't deny it."

Patrick was referring to an attack by a knife wielding gang on himself and his friends, many years before, when he lived in England. In a struggle with one of the men, Patrick had been wounded but the other man died, stabbed by his own knife. It was the reason why James McGrother had never wanted his daughter to marry Patrick, and Thomas was beginning to wonder if his father had been right in his thinking at the time.

"Surely we could have tied him up and gagged him to give us enough time to get away?" challenged Thomas.

"How long do you think it would have been until someone discovered him? Even if we had made it onto the stage, the sheriff and his deputies would have caught up with us before we ever had a chance to board a train." Patrick grabbed a fistful of his brother-in-law's shirt and

138

pulled him close, "I had to act quickly because of your stupidity. Besides, it was you that hit him over the head in the first place. So you share as much of the blame as I do."

Their noses just inches apart, Thomas felt stifled and pulled back. There was such venom in Patrick's voice, he feared he might push him from the moving train in a fit of rage. The alarm must have been obvious on Thomas's face and Patrick quickly released him.

"As you said yourself, I do not display any remorse. But that does not mean I have none. We must put this behind us or it will destroy our friendship."

Thomas looked at the hand being offered to him. The hurt in his companion's eyes conveyed the sincerity of his words but it wasn't enough to completely erase his feelings of apprehension. Nevertheless, he took hold of Patrick's hand with a firm grasp.

One look at his friends' faces as they returned to their seats was enough to tell Petey they had made a truce, of sorts. There was still a slight aloofness between them but at least they were now on speaking terms and the atmosphere had become much more amicable.

"You are more than welcome to stay with us, Petey, when we arrive in New York. We'll squeeze you in somewhere," Patrick offered.

"There is a bed to spare at my apartment and Lily would be more than happy to have you as our guest," said Thomas.

Petey looked from one man to the other and felt torn between them. He tried to decide which one would be most offended if he declined their offer. In the end, he thought of a good compromise.

139

"Is Catherine still as good a cook as I remember her being?" Petey inquired of Patrick.

"Even better. Why do you ask?"

"If it's not too much trouble for the both of ye, I could have my meals at your home and my night's sleep at Thomas's – just until I have earned the price of a passage back to Ireland."

"That's fair enough, Petey," said Patrick, "We'll not fall out over it. Shall we, Thomas?"

CHAPTER TWENTY-THREE

Jamie hadn't touched a drop of the tea his mother-in-law poured for him. Annie, on the other hand, couldn't stop drinking hers. She stood to replenish her cup and heard a loud squawking of hens outside the door. It was then she noticed her mother had not fully closed it when she left to give them some privacy.

"You can go now, Ma. He's not going to break any of your crockery," Annie shouted from the stove, her back to the door.

The clucking of the hens faded as they followed Annie's mother away from the house. Jamie watched his wife cross the room to fully close the door and his mouth went dry. He emptied most of his tea in one gulp, wishing it was a different beverage altogether; one that would give him more courage.

The caustic reception Jamie had received from both his wife and her mother almost made him turn tail and run. The only reason he stood his ground on the doorstep, was the fear of someone finding out about it. That same fear had forced him to walk the two miles to his in-laws' house, three days after his row with Annie.

Each morning, Jamie had returned to his cottage after a night of fishing, fully expecting his wife to be back in her own home. As the days dragged on, he finally conceded that Annie was even more stubborn than himself. The young husband had begun to worry that the neighbours would start making up their own stories as to her disappearance. As it was, Jamie inwardly cringed every time he received a knowing glance to his explanation for her absence.

"Half the parish thinks we have a baby on the way," Jamie blurted out.

"They do? I wonder what has them thinking that, now. Would it have anything to do with you telling the neighbours I've been ailing?"

"What was I supposed to tell them? My wife stormed off in a temper and left me after a few months of being wed?" Jamie picked up his cup and realised it was empty.

Annie noted his discomfort, "I'll fetch you another sup of tea."

While her back was turned to her husband, she allowed herself a tiny smile of satisfaction. It was not her intention to hurt his pride, nor humiliate him. Annie believed their first big row would set the pattern for those to come and she had married a strong-willed man.

"You must be starving, do you want a cut of bread? I made some for Ma this morning," Annie placed the hot tea on the table as she sat opposite her husband.

"I'm grand. Rosie next door gave me a round of bread yesterday along with a pot of soup."

It was Annie's turn to feel uncomfortable, "I suppose she's been feeling sorry for you, has she? What have you been telling her? That I'm a poor wife to you?"

Jamie was taken aback at the accusation, "I told her what I've been telling everyone asking about your absence – that you've not been well of late."

"I wouldn't like you to be talking about our problems to others, Jamie."

"You told your mother about the broken cup, did you not?"

Annie smiled. "And the plate. I heard it hit the wall," she moved to the chair next to Jamie's. "I meant others *outside* of the family. It's only natural that a woman should turn to her mother in times of trouble."

"I suppose you're right. I've seen that with my own sisters and I've confided in my father once or twice, myself," Jamie replied, pleased that his wife had moved closer to him.

Annie took a deep breath and hoped for the best, "Speaking of sisters, I'm not giving up my work, Jamie," she avoided using the name that would sour the moment.

Jamie gave a quick glance at both windows in the kitchen, front and back of the house, for fear someone may be watching.

"If you want me to beg you to give up that work, I'll get down on my knees this very minute," Jamie began to push his chair back from the table.

"No, don't do that. Never do such a thing," Annie began to cry, "The man I love would never beg anything from anyone. Oh, what am I doing to you?"

Holding his wife in his arms, Jamie felt his confidence in their relationship return. He tried his best to make himself feel less hostile towards Mary-Anne but it was no good.

"Would it bother you as much if I were to bake some goods to sell to your sister," Annie tried for a compromise, "I could even prepare the meals for her guests in my own kitchen for her to collect."

"You have no need to be working, Annie, I'm well able to provide for us."

"I know you are, Jamie, but I want to earn my own wee bit of a wage. I can put it by for the days when you cannot bring the boat out and there's no labouring to be had."

There was a moment of silence and Annie prayed her words would have a positive effect.

"Is there no other work to be found in the whole village, Annie?"

"Only scrubbing and cleaning and emptying chamber pots, Jamie, and there's plenty already doing that. Your sister never asked me to do such chores. It's my cooking she's paying me for."

"I have no wish to have that woman anywhere near my home, Annie, so you will have to deliver the meals to her yourself. That is, if she agrees with the arrangement."

"She will, Jamie, I'm sure of it," Annie was beaming.

"But you must promise never to set foot in her house when you go there."

It was a relief to the young man to see his wife back to her old self and Jamie stood to lead her towards the door, "I think I would rather be in our own kitchen right now, Annie. Go and say goodbye to your ma from me, love. I'm not sure I want to face her just yet."

CHAPTER TWENTY-FOUR

As they walked across the hard, damp sand of Blackrock's beach, George ran ahead of James and Mary, balancing a sliotar on his hurley as he went.

"He has the makings of a fine hurler, Mary. It was well worth my time carving that stick for him. Look at how well he carries himself."

"You sound like a mighty proud grandfather, James McGrother."

"I am, indeed. Sure, he's as good as flesh and blood to us, is he not?"

In the short time he had been with them, young George captured the hearts of the McGrother family to such an extent, that his adoptive grandparents felt as if he had always been part of their lives. Mary-Anne made no effort to encourage the young boy to participate in any kind of sport. Instead, he was to bury his head in a book at every opportunity. She had big plans for George and didn't want him getting side-tracked by overindulgence in something she considered a wasteful expenditure of time and energy.

"It's a pity the poor boy must hide his talent from his mother," tutted Mary, "I think I shall have to give our Mary-Anne a bit of a talking to."

"I wouldn't waste my breath. No, love, best leave it. George knows he can behave like a young boy when he is in our company and we shall just have to make do with that, for now. Besides, from what I hear, Mary-Anne might have a suitor," James smiled knowingly at his wife. "With a man to distract her, she might be less strict on the boy."

"Are you speaking of Sergeant Broderick? Sure, that's only old talk. He's nearly as ancient as ourselves, James. Anyways, our Mary-Anne has never shown much interest in men, I always said she'd be a spinster in her old age – and look how well she's done for herself, in spite of it, or because of it."

"I take it you're of the opinion that having a husband does a woman no favours, so."

Mary detected a slight edge in James's tone, "I said no such thing, but now you mention it, I suppose the same goes for men who choose not to burden themselves with a wife and children," she speculated.

"I have never once, in all our years together, thought of you or the children as burdens. Having a family to provide for can be the makings of a man. Women are more likely to save their money and spend it wisely," James patted the back of his wife's hand. "Maybe what you say about Mary-Anne is true but it was our Jamie that told me of the sergeant's intentions towards her. I was told that in confidence, mind, so don't you go telling anyone about it – especially not Maggie."

"If Jamie told you, then there must be something to it. He's not one for idle chatter," Mary had a worried look on her face. "Keep an eye on that man, James, he could be out to take advantage of our daughter. Mary-Anne is very innocent where men are concerned."

James was beginning to regret confiding in his wife but before he could promise to keep an eye on Sergeant Broderick, a woman shouted from behind them. They turned to see her running with a piece of paper in her hand.

"It's Mrs. Halpin. I hope she has not received bad news," said Mary.

"It cannot be that bad, with the smile she has on her face."

By the time Mrs. Halpin reached them she was out of breath and it took her a few seconds to compose herself, "It's a telegram from America. Our Petey has been found safe and sound."

"Oh that's great news altogether," Mary hugged the excited woman, while James patted her on the back.

"There's a letter on its way with more news for us. Would you read it to us when it comes, James? After all, it was you who wrote to Thomas and asked for his help. I cannot thank you enough, God bless you and your fine son."

James felt very uncomfortable as Petey's mother grabbed his hand and kissed the back of it. "There's no need for that at all, Mrs. Halpin. Sure, it was only a letter. It's Thomas that found him, by the sound of it."

Mary caught hold of the woman's arm and led her away from James and his discomfort.

"Keep an eye on young George, while I bring Mrs. Halpin over to our Mary-Anne's for a cup of tea. Bring the boy home when he's tired himself out, love."

James breathed a sigh of relief as the two women walked arm in arm back towards the main street. Although he understood the reason for such gratitude bestowed on him by Petey's mother, he hoped it was not something she would be repeating too often and certainly not in public. Nevertheless, James's curiosity was piqued by the prospect of a letter, hopefully written by Thomas, revealing the events that led to discovering the young man's whereabouts.

Later that evening, when Maggie and their granddaughter, Eliza, had gone to their beds in the small back room, James and Mary sat by the stove. They still enjoyed the pleasure of each other's company, even after many years of marriage.

Having spoken again of Mary-Anne's supposed suitor and how it might affect George, James managed to extract a promise from his wife that she would give it more time before broaching the subject with their daughter.

"Life is good for us at present, James. Do you not think so?" Mary sighed contentedly.

"It is, love. That last letter from Catherine had nothing but good news in it. Young Tom, an apprentice and the girls doing well with their schooling. Let us enjoy these good times, Mary, while they last."

"Aye, that's true enough," Mary took hold of James's hand, "I'm thankful to have Mary-Anne back home again, and now we have two fine grandchildren with us. Although, there's no telling how long it will be until Eliza joins her father in America."

"Ach, Mary. You've been saying that since Thomas wed Lily, and it hasn't happened as yet. Sure, didn't we always say that our Breege would be off to America the first chance she got? And where is she now? Working in a big house in Dublin – I could carry you there on my back, if I had to," James leaned across to plant a kiss on Mary's cheek, "Let's not worry ourselves about things that might never happen."

"I'm sorry for being so maudlin, love. Tell me a story from your childhood, James, one that will make me laugh. I like that one of the time yourself and Michael Kiernan got drunk on whiskey, when ye were no bigger than young George."

******

In Patrick Gallagher's home, in the city of New York, a very different story was passed on to another branch of the McGrother family. It was one of danger and intrigue. Petey Halpin said very little, which was unusual for him, as he watched his two friends answer questions from their wives.

Thomas lay his young adopted son across his lap and rocked him to sleep as he recounted their adventures. Every so often, Lily rubbed his back, as if assuring herself that she was not in a dream and imagining his presence.

Patrick was also quiet, happy to let his brother-in-law do all the talking. His daughters shared his lap while Catherine stood behind, leaning against the back of his chair, her hands resting on his shoulders. Whenever Thomas came to a particularly gripping episode, embellished somewhat by his dramatic storytelling, the girls would shriek and bury their heads in their father's chest.

As the tension in the room heightened, Catherine's fingers dug into her husband's flesh. Although they were listening to a censored version of the story, on account of the children being present, it was still enough to upset her. When Patrick leaned his head back to smile up at her, Catherine cupped his face in her hands and planted a kiss on his forehead.

Young Tom sat next to Petey, enthralled by his uncle's words. He had to remind himself that he was not listening to an adventure being read to them from a book of fiction.

"You must have been in fear for your life," Tom whispered to their guest.

"I was, many a time," Petey replied. "I cannot thank your father and your uncle enough, for rescuing me."

Observing the happy faces of the two families, reunited with their men, Petey realised just how much of a risk Patrick and Thomas had taken. If their plans had not succeeded, their wives may have been widowed and their children left fatherless. The young man's appreciation grew as the evening wore on and he silently vowed to do everything in his power to repay them at some point in the future.

As the urge to return to his own family grew stronger by the minute, Petey visualized the moment he would step off the boat in Dundalk, to be crushed in his brothers' arms and embarrassed by his mother's hot tears against his cheek. He had enough stories in him to entertain the men in Paddy Mac's for years to come and if they managed to capture the heart of a fine young woman, then his adventure and the hardship that came with it, would have been worth every second.

Patrick noticed how withdrawn Petey had become and leaned sideways to speak to him.

"Are you thinking of your own family, by any chance. I'm sorry if we're making you feel homesick, Petey, but it won't be too long now before you're on a ship to Ireland."

"I know, Patrick. I shall save every cent until I have the fare. My return will be like that parable in the gospel won't it? The one about the Prodigal Son," Petey smiled. "I was thinking of all my adventures since I got here and the stories I'll have to tell when I get home. Do you think women might find that sort of thing appealing?"

Patrick laughed quietly, so as not to divert the attention from Thomas.

"Well now," he whispered, "If it's a woman you're in search of I'll not be surprised to hear you've gotten yourself into another pile of trouble, but don't count on me coming to your rescue again, Petey." Patrick's eyes lingered on Catherine, who had moved to the other side of the room to set the kettle on the hotplate. "There are some troubles a man would give his right arm to hold on to," he said wistfully.

As she turned to announce that supper was almost ready, Catherine caught Patrick's gaze and returned his smile. She then gave him a secret sign that only he would understand, an assurance that he had a night of love ahead of him.

"Aye, Petey, the kind of trouble a man would give up his life for."

THE END

(Book 6 to follow)

References

Chapter 1

Orphan Trains
Over 250,000 children were transported from New York to the Midwest, over a 75-year period (1854-1929) in the largest mass migration of children in American history. As many as one in four were Irish.
http://irishamerica.com/2014/03/the-orphan-trains/

Chapter 5

Tammany Hall
Tammany Hall, also known as the Society of St. Tammany, was a New York City political organization founded in 1786 and incorporated on May 12, 1789, as the Tammany Society. It eventually became the Democratic Party political machine that played a major role in controlling New York City and New York State politics and helping immigrants, most notably the Irish, rise up in American politics.

Tammany's control over the politics of New York City tightened considerably under William (Boss) Tweed during the 1860's. Tweed knew that his constituents' support was necessary for him to remain in power, and he used the machinery of the city's government to provide social services, which included the building of orphanages, alms houses and public baths.

When "Honest" John Kelly assumed control in 1871 after a disgraced Tweed was thrown into prison for political corruption, he turned

Tammany into an organisation that became a cohesive force in New York politics. Its structure began to mirror the organisation of which the vast majority of its members and supporters also subscribed to, the Catholic Church. https://en.wikipedia.org/wiki/William_M._Tweed

Chapter 11

Runners
Runners were Irishmen who spoke to the new arrivals from Ireland in their own tongue. These passengers were often confused and suffering from culture shock in cities such as New York and Boston and happy to be pointed in what they believed to be the right direction. In truth, they were conned and often thrown into the streets, their luggage and possessions confiscated, when their money was eaten up by grossly inflated rent. These runners also made their way out to the ships quarantined in the bay, in their effort to find vulnerable Irish immigrants. Often, they worked in league with so-called 'forwarding agents' selling fake or used rail and boat tickets, usually at scandalously high prices.
You can read more about this on the following website:

http://www.historyplace.com/worldhistory/famine/america.htm

Chapter 15

Camán is the Irish word for a hurley stick.
Sliotar is the hard leather ball, used in the game.

Iománaíocht is the Irish word for the game of hurling.

Infernal Machines
Infernal machines or dynamite bombs, as they were called, held the potential to arm thousands of Fenians thus removing past dependency on foreign powers for the provision of weapons. You can read more about them here:

http://www.historyireland.com/18th-19th-century-history/scientific-warfare-or-the-quickest-way-to-liberate-ireland-the-brooklyn-dynamite-school/

Chapter 16

The inspiration for the fictional account of Heartless Hannigan came from a tragic event that occurred in Pennsylvania in 1832. Fifty-seven Irish railroad workers suffering from cholera near Malvern, Pennsylvania were apparently refused medical attention. They died and were buried in an unmarked mass grave, barely six weeks after their arrival in America. An investigation into their deaths, on what was called *Duffy's Cut*, led to the discovery of some of their remains. The first to be found was that of 18 year old John Ruddy, who was identified by DNA testing, and his remains were returned to his family in Ardara, Co. Donegal in 2013. If you search for *Duffy's Cut* on Youtube, you'll find some eye-opening documentaries about the tragedy. This article in *The Irish Examiner* gives a very detailed account of the incident and a timeline of events:

http://www.irishexaminer.com/lifestyle/features/blood-on-the-tracks-were-50-irish-immigrants-murdered-in-philadelphia-in-1832-268069.html

Author Bio

Jean Reinhardt was born in Louth, grew up in Dublin and lived in Alicante, Spain for almost eight years. With five children and three grandchildren, life is never dull. She now lives in Ireland and loves to read, write, listen to music and spend time with family and friends. When Jean isn't writing she likes to take long walks through the woods and on the beach.

Jean writes poetry, short stories and novels. Her favourite genres are Young Adult and Historical Fiction.

Twitter:
https://twitter.com/JeanReinhardt1

Facebook:
https://www.facebook.com/JeanReinhardtWriter/

Website/Blog:
https://jeanreinhardt.wordpress.com/

Amazon Author Page:
https://www.amazon.com/Jean-Reinhardt/e/B00CSMF0VW

Other books by the author:

A Pocket Full of Shells (Book 1: An Irish Family Saga)
A Year of Broken Promises (Book 2: An Irish Family Saga)

A Turning of the Tide (Book 3: An Irish Family Saga)

A Legacy of Secrets (Book 4: An Irish Family Saga)

The Finding Trilogy: a young adult medical thriller.

Book 1: *Finding Kaden*

Book 2: *Finding Megan*

Book 3: *Finding Henry Brubaker*

All books are in digital and paperback format on Amazon and Smashwords. They can also be ordered from The Book Depository and Createspace.

Acknowledgements

As always, I'm extremely grateful to my beta readers for taking on the early drafts and giving me their honest feedback; Anne, Carol, Dana, Kevin, Grace, Brenda, Eileen, Jeannine, Kitty, Ellen, Peter, Ann, Maureen, Pamela and Vera.

Front cover image – the author's father, Jack as a child, and his mother, Edna Parker.

I would be tearing my hair out if it wasn't for my husband untangling the technical mess I get myself into while formatting these books. Thanks for helping me out, Bob Reinhardt.

Many thanks to Noel Sharkey (historian and poet) who is always so encouraging and supportive.

The following books proved to be a great source of information in the writing of this story. They are full of well documented events and photographs of people whose families have lived in Blackrock for many generations, including my own:

The Parish of Haggardstown & Blackrock – A History by Noel Sharkey.
First Printed in 2003 by Dundalgan Press (W. Tempest) Ltd., Dundalk.

The Parish of Haggardstown & Blackrock – A Pictorial Record
Compiled and written by Noel Sharkey with photos by Owen Byrne.
Printed in 2008 by Dundalgan Press (W. Tempest) Ltd., Dundalk.

70636706R00096

Made in the USA
Columbia, SC
10 May 2017